A Year

Maddie Grigg was born creative writing course, w ... local newspaper editor Margery Hookings studied as part of her honours degree. Since then, Maddie has gained a loyal following for her blog, *The World from My Window*, which takes an affectionate and amusing look at country life in Dorset and Corfu. Maddie/Margery is married with two children, three step-children, five grandchildren and lives in a permanent state of anxiety.

A Year in Lush Places
Tales from England's rural underbelly

Maddie Grigg

Published in 2013 by FeedARead.com Publishing – Arts Council funded

Copyright © Maddie Grigg.

The author or authors assert their moral right under the Copyright, Designs and Patents Act, 1988, to be identified as the author or authors of this work.

All Rights reserved. No part of this publication may be reproduced, copied, stored in a retrieval system, or transmitted, in any form or by any means, without the prior written consent of the copyright holder, nor be otherwise circulated in any form of binding or cover other than that in which it is published and without a similar condition being imposed on the subsequent purchaser.

A CIP catalogue record for this title is available from the British Library.

What people are saying about *A Year in Lush Places*:

A Diary of a Nobody for the 21st Century.
P. Sheepwash

She's captured me perfectly.
C. Charlie

English eccentricity at its best.
F M Putter

A sort of Tom Sharpe meets Thomas Hardy in the post office queue.
Sheba Bancroft

Completely bonkers but I love her.
B Grigg

To my friends in Lush Places
and especially to Mr Grigg and Mrs Bancroft
for making Lush Places so lush

'Such casual collection of data is pleasant and sociable but often unreliable. But if the personal is fallible, it is also organic. There is no life without it.'
Dr Thomas Fuller, 1608-1661

Author's note

Once upon a time, I began to write about the place in Dorset where I live. It's a quirky little village where the weird and wonderful happens all the time. Google chose my online diary, *The World from My Window*, as a Blog of Note and it attracted a huge following. I even had a pair of Canadian ladies turn up at my front door for a tour of Lush Places. Ever polite, I invited them in for a cup of tea but I drew the line at showing them around the village when they complained about the cake and said my house was rather small.

You, however, are different.

So, let me take you by the hand as I escort you around Lush Places, an enchanted village where the London blow-ins seldom venture, where the mist swirls around and around the top of Bluebell Hill like a maelstrom and where the village, like ancient Sparta only not as aggressive, is a law unto itself. Stay with me for twelve months, let's say the year 2010, to get to know my friends and neighbours. I hope they will forgive me for taking more than a few liberties. For example, I don't think Champagne-Charlie has ever taken out a street light with a shotgun (although we all wish he would). And I have never ever been jealous of Posh Totty (well, maybe just once or twice).

This is a work of fiction but very much anchored in real life: Lush Places and the people in it really exist. Only the names have been changed to protect the guilty.

Maddie Grigg
May 2013

Prologue

I climb a narrow staircase to look out of a bedroom window onto a village square, with a red telephone box, an old water pump, a corner shop, a pub and a village green. It is peaceful, quiet. I watch as the paper boy props his bike up against the kerb and ambles, ape-like, into the shop. In headphone oblivion, he does not hear the crash when the bike tips into the road.

The driver of the Land Rover that comes tearing around the corner doesn't see the bike either. There is a metallic scrunching sound and a crowd appears from nowhere. In unison, people emerge from their front doors, put their hands over their mouths and then scratch their heads. An old man with a beard prods the mangled bicycle with the hooked end of a curly walking stick and tries to retrieve it from the Land Rover's undercarriage. Another man with a twirly pipe hanging from his mouth grabs the handlebars in an attempt to pull the bike out.

The Land Rover driver shrugs, goes into the shop to get the *Daily Mail*, comes back out again and gets behind the wheel. He starts the engine, disengages the handbrake and, with a crunch, the Land Rover wheels go up and then over the bike, which is taken along for the ride like a modern art version of bull bars.

The paperboy comes out of the shop with a bag of sweets, mounts a non-existent bike and gets five yards down the road before realising it isn't there.

And then a ginger wig rolls by like tumbleweed as the church clock strikes thirteen.

From the warmth of the room, I feel a hand on my shoulder.

Mr Grigg.

'What do you think?' he says to me, as I gaze out of the window, an estate agent with a clipboard behind him. 'Should we buy the house?'

'I'm sold,' I say.

And that is how we came to be living right here in the heart of Lush Places.

Chapter 1

January

1 January: Mr Grigg is lying in bed, high up in the eaves. My eyes are closed but I know he's looking at me. In my head I can hear the strains of Ian Dury's *Wake Up and Make Love With Me*. I picture Mr Grigg's fleshy shoulders, the grey hairs standing out on his chest and a smutty smirk on his big moon face. He is sitting up and he reaches out to me with his right arm. He may even still be wearing his black Stetson. I can almost hear his mind um-ing and ah-ing as he considers whether to prod me in the back with his plastic Colt 45. He decides against it.

'Happy New Year to you baby,' he coos.

I keep my eyes firmly shut. He turns over, and sighs as big as Devon.

And as the houses around us come to life, the scenes are playing out in my head like a film montage just as the introductory, on-screen credits roll. Each character has their own piece of music to identify them. (Remember that, because it will give you the same picture as I have every time I meet them. And if you don't know the music, go on YouTube, the world's greatest free jukebox).

Across the road in Lush Places, Mrs Bancroft (*Arrival of the Queen of Sheba*) lifts her eye shades as she wakes up to Sky News and a nice cup of tea in a bone china mug with a pink flower pattern on it.

Next door, Mrs Bubbles Champagne-Charlie, is hung over.

'What are you *doing* Charles?' she says from the comfort of crisp, white bed linen and through squinted eyes. She fumbles on the bedside cabinet for her spectacles and knocks over a glass of water. Mr Champagne-Charlie (*The Liquidator*) is in striped pyjamas and kneeling at the sash window. Unlike Mr Grigg, he has a real shotgun, which is pointing towards the street light outside.

'Bloody thing,' he says. 'There's too much sodding light in here.' So he fires both barrels at the lamp post and their bedroom is plunged into darkness.

'That's better,' he says, and gets back into bed.

Down the road, Pelly and Mr Sheepwash (*There Ain't Half Been Some Clever Bastards*) are sitting up in bed listening to Radio 4 and reading *The Guardian* while a gaggle of grown-up children snore loudly in the many-bedded house.

Up at the love shack, Mr Loggins (*Night Boat to Cairo*) is doing a keep-fit circuit around the perimeter while his wife, Darling, sits up on her pillows, wearing bed-jacket and tightly buttoned-up nightie, and calls for her Tigger of a husband to come back under the covers.

'That'll keep you fit,' she says.

Meanwhile, Celebrity Farmer (*Gonna Make You a Star*) walks up and down the cow stalls in his blue overalls and turns on his heels as if he is on the catwalk in Milan. He speaks into a bottle of iodine and does a running commentary while the milking machines go swish-swish-swish and his older brother shakes his head.

And then the clip-clop, clip-clop of Posh Totty on horseback, riding through the street, sends all the men running to their bedroom windows to gaze out and swoon. The women give a collective harrumph, swing their legs and get out of bed.

Just another morning in The Enchanted Village.

4 January: Mr Grigg calls me his little Madam Butterfly because I flit from project to project, with the latest manuscript always being 'the next big thing'. But my words invariably end up in a large shoe box, three-quarters finished. My characters are frozen in time, waiting to be released. It's as if I were just a little bit scared of getting to the end and then someone telling me to go right back and start again. I am surrounded by boxes of stories that are not-quite-there-yet, incomplete novels, ideas not fledged enough to fly the nest. My characters bother me in my sleep, pulling at my pyjamas. 'You can't leave me like this,' they whine. But I do. Oh, such power. Such powerless power.

And Mr Grigg, he just smiles and says: 'One day, baby, one day.'

My computer is on a desk in the smaller of the two bedrooms. I am trying to write a novel. It's about a time travelling prostitute. It seemed like a good idea at the time, until I got a third of the way through and found out someone had got there first with a book called *My Little Dirty Book of Stolen Time.* I just wanted to find out where the author lived and go and punch her on the nose. Bitch. So I sit at the computer monitor, with its star-field screensaver blinding me. It's too busy and it's annoying me. So I press on a key to stop the damn thing and up jumps an advert for Google Blogger: 'Create your own blog'. So I mess about a bit, choose a template and start writing.

I look out of the window onto my world.

It is morning and the ginger wig I have grown to know and love blows past the window and shoots up Church Path. I can see a man fly-fishing in a field behind the allotments. And the paper boy comes nose-to-nose with a blow-up reindeer as it re-inflates itself on the front wall of a house still bedecked with Christmas lights.

Then it dawns on me. Who needs a time travelling prostitute when you've got this on your doorstep?

6 January: Mr Grigg is a bit of a Western freak. He sees himself as something of a cross between Clint Eastwood and *The Virginian,* although he looks more like Dan Blocker, who played Hoss in *Bonanza*. And then there's Mr Sheepwash, whose favourite film of all time is *Shane*, which is interesting considering he is such an intellectual. Mr Loggins is more of a *Deputy Dawg* man while Mr Champagne-Charlie could be straight from the campfire scene in *Blazing Saddles*. You know, the one where the after-effects of eating baked beans ripples around and gains its own momentum.

On New Year's Eve for I don't know how many years running, we've had a Wild West night in the village hall. One year Mr Grigg decided to go as Howard Keel so he and six others could cart off seven women.

I worry about him. He claims to adore me but he has a roving eye. My mother used to call him The Philanderer. And leopards don't change their spots.

Still, he married me, didn't he? So why should I worry?

10 January: Outside my window this morning the square is full of people on horseback. There is a man in toff's yellow trousers, the colour of calf-scour, running around topping up people's glasses. And there's a woman who looks a bit like Delia Smith serving up light bites on a silver tray. It's Mr and Mrs Champagne-Charlie, hosting the annual meet of the local hunt.

People are lining the pavements, dressed in new hats and gloves they have been given for Christmas. A man in a red coat atop a very tall horse comes down the one-way system, surrounded by foxhounds in the way flies buzz around a cow pat. I'm sitting in the bedroom window, away from the action as a matter of principle but armed with a camera and a telephoto lens. And then I see her. On a black horse, a very attractive woman a little bit younger than me and with a roll of auburn hair in a hairnet under a velvet riding hat. She looks down for a tray to place the stirrup cup. Six men come from nowhere to help. Mr Grigg, still chomping on a sausage roll, gets there first.

'Let me take that, my dear,' he says, in a voice rather too posh from a man originally from Bristol.

I zoom in with my camera lens. The woman looks down her aquiline nose and smiles with lips rather too made-up for a day following the hounds. Mr Grigg beams as he takes her cup.

'Bottoms up,' she says in a crystal glass voice.

'You bet,' says a still beaming Mr Grigg.

Posh Totty smiles as she turns her horse, which flicks its tail across Mr Grigg's great moon face. He is smitten. I take a picture.

Bastard.

The horses part like the Red Sea as a young red-haired farmer drives through the square on his large tractor and does a royal wave.

'Wasn't that the chap in *Band of Brothers*?' I hear someone on the pavement saying to their companion.

'What, Damian Lewis? No, that's Celebrity Farmer,' says Mr Loggins, butting in.

As the hunt trots off into the distance and onlookers disperse, Mr Grigg picks up a shovel he prepared earlier, in anticipation of his prize, scoops up the horse muck and puts it on the passion flower outside our house.

'You've missed a bit,' I say from on high, pointing to a pile of poo outside the shop.

'Oh hello baby,' he says, looking up 'I didn't know you were up there. You should have been down here with everyone else.'

'I don't think so, do you?' I say. 'It's *hunting*.'

We don't agree on many things, Mr Grigg and me. Sometimes I'm surprised we ever got together.

11 January: It is one of those lovely winter days, with a low sun and cold wind. It is muddy underfoot and the chill air gets to your cheekbones. The children squeal in the playground before school begins, as a playground supervisor called Bellows obliterates the morning call of Russell's Crow, the cockerel across the valley.

The sky to the west this morning is like a painting by a Dutch old master. In the early evening, Venus leads the charge to make way for an incredible array of stars and the waning Wolf Moon of January.

Mr Grigg comes home from the last shoot of the season, sloshing with a belly full of port and cider, a grin across his big face and a huge hole in the gusset of his boxer shorts. He is desperate to be taken seriously as a countryman. Although Bristol is the West Country, it could just as well be Mars as far as the locals are concerned. It's not Dorset. And for all his Wild West bravado, he can't even ride.

12 January: We've been stripping paint off a wood panelled wall in our little cottage. We have lived here for five years now but the place still isn't finished. The dust is getting to us, so we saunter across the square for a pint. Mr Grigg is still wearing his face mask but on top of his hairline, so it's like a white clown's little pointed hat, a codpiece for the forehead. As usual, the village is swirling in mist, and we're at the top of the beanstalk in a giant's land. Before we get to the pub, we suddenly hear what sounds like a ship's horn from up the road, which is odd because we're seven miles inland. Mr Loggins comes cycling down the one-way system at a rate of knots, blowing his nose, and looking for something to do after a twenty-mile ride on his mountain bike.

'I've just passed the most fabulous oak tree on Bluebell Hill,' he says. 'Dead as a doornail. Be great for burning. Wouldn't take much to shift it.'

So Mr Grigg and Mr Loggins are off in an instant, to examine the spoils and plan their escape route. They rope in Mr Sheepwash as a getaway driver. For an intellectual he is very easily led.

So I'm left on my own, a logging widow, and go over to the pub for a pint and a pie with Pelly Sheepwash who wins a rib of beef on the meat draw and gives it to me because she's a vegetarian.

15 January: There is a bronze statue in the front garden of a 1980s house at the entrance to our enchanted village. We call her the nymph. She stands in a pile of rocks, hands and arms outstretched as if in a yoga prayer, her nakedness on show to all (including passing schoolchildren, which greatly upset Mrs Bancroft). Today the nymph could really do with a bit more clothing. It's very cold. Maybe she should be wearing a hat or something. Or possibly Mr St John's shorts.

Speak of the devil. My attention is drawn away from the nymph when I see Mr St John slinking up to the shop for his paper. For some reason, James Brown's *Papa's Got A Brand New Bag* jerks its way into my head. He strolls athletically, in yellow polo shirt, navy shorts and flip flops. *Flip flops*. It's the middle of bloody winter.

As he passes Mrs Bancroft's house, he looks in the window to admire his own reflection.

But Mrs Bancroft is at the sink, up to her neck in Fairy Liquid, wearing rubber gloves with a fur trim and staring out in a sort of trance. She waves a dishcloth as Mr St John passes and he does a double take when he realises he has been spotted.

I go for a double whammy, and open my window and shout: 'Coo-eeee!' He looks suitably embarrassed, mutters something I can't quite make out and slopes off into the shop to the sound of the James Brown horn section.

18 January: I am scrawling in my writer's notebook in the lavatory during a supper party at Ted Moult and Jamie Lee's. Jamie is with our neighbour, Bubbles, in the kitchen. They are fussing around in a Delia-Smith-meets-mother-hen-kind-of-way with a coffee machine shaped like a chicken as the guests relax after a cracking meal of belly pork. I've had to excuse myself as I'm a bit taken aback because Posh Totty (*Black Magic Woman*) has just peeled off her jeans at the dinner table to show Mr Grigg a bruise on her thigh caused by an excited horse. I console myself by gazing at her rather handsome husband, MDF Man, in a soft focus of red-wine.

The horse, it seems, was not the only one excited by Posh Totty's thighs. On seeing Mr Grigg's reaction, I coughed loudly and he quickly put his tongue back in his mouth.

Drooling is not a good look for a person approaching sixty from the wrong direction.

Posh Totty has the most wonderful figure, dazzling blue eyes and an accent that would be perfectly at ease at a Buckingham Palace banquet. She is charming, the loveliest person you could meet and I hate her.

While I am thinking voodoo thoughts as I come back from the lavatory, the entire dinner party is dazzled by the headlights of a car being driven up and down the drive by Mr St John. He is trying to work out who's been invited to dinner because he hasn't.

A little later on, another guest, Camilla, generously gives me her button necklace after I remark for the fourth time and after the third glass of Sauvignon Blanc how pretty it is, while her husband, Mr F Word, and Mr Grigg discuss recipes, swearing and football.

I try to foist it back on her. 'Honestly,' I say, embarrassed. 'I didn't mean you had to *give* it to me.'

'Oh take it,' she says, practically ripping it off. 'I don't really like it. I'd much rather *you* had it.'

On our way back, Mr Grigg and I do a tango across the village square.

'It's a marvellous night for a moondance,' says Mr Grigg and threatens to drop his trousers, which is his idea of a play on words.

It's all very well being married to someone larger than life. But sometimes I don't feel big enough to cope.

In the bedroom, we try to undress in a drunken haze. Mr Grigg's leg gets caught in his boxer shorts, he falls to the floor with a huge thump. I try to help him but have troubles of my own. The button necklace I have been given by Camilla is wrapped so tightly around my neck I can't get it off. Mr Grigg attempts to unravel it for me, while I fight off a panic attack, imaging I am from ancient Greece mythology and struggling to fight off an incendiary dress and coronet. Tonight, I christen this new piece of jewellery The Medea Necklace.

22 January: In the blogging world, there is a thing in which you are meant to give an insight into yourself by answering a few questions, sharing the answers with the blogosphere and then passing it on to some unlucky bastard who has to do the same. It's a bit like a chain letter and I don't like it. However, for the purposes of telling you more about myself, it's a quite useful tool, so here goes:

Obsessions?
1. To be a successful writer while working in an office I hate.
2. Music. From jazz to trip-hop, Westcountry folk songs, ska and the theme to *Gladiator*, there's nothing much I don't like. Each person in my blog has a theme tune.
3. Mr Grigg (*Just a Gigolo*)
4. Can I trust him?

Which item from your wardrobe do you wear most often?
My red beret. When I was slimmer I used to look like a Swan Vesta.

What's for dinner?
Rabbit casserole. Our neighbour Mr Champagne-Charlie has just bagged a couple of bunnies on the cricket pitch while Mr Grigg held his gun case.

Last thing you bought?
1. A top in the White Stuff sale. When Mr Grigg sees it I'll tell him I've had it for ages. I've earned my own money for thirty years and still feel guilty when I spend it.
2. Six oranges, four apples and some Fair Trade bananas.
3. Boots Evening Primrose moisturiser and some deodorant that's not meant to leave white marks *but it bloody does*.

What are you listening to?
A Louis Prima compilation. The voice of King Louie in *The Jungle Book*.

Loveliest locations?
1. Ithaca - I love all things Greek but especially Ithaca. Its very name makes me tingle with Homeric joy. Home is very important to me and so is Homer. And Mr Grigg is like Homer Simpson.
2. New York - a living film set. I would be a very attractive high flyer with superpowers and high heels. But with a long body and short legs, it's not the best combination.
3. Ireland - I love the scenery of the west coast, the spontaneity, the friendliness and the craic.

Reading right now?
1. *The Time Traveller's Wife* by Audrey Niffenegger
2. Simon Schama's *History of Britain* (I bought the three volumes for £3 at a book sale. I dip in and out of them but it's more fun when you do it out of chronological order).

Four words to describe yourself.
Quirky, determined, cynical, tired.

Guilty pleasure?
Galaxy chocolate under my Primark blanky after nine o'clock at night.

Who or what makes you laugh until you're weak?
Peter Kay, Tom Sharpe and Mr Grigg.

Heroine?
Marge Simpson. Such patience and wisdom. Great hair too.

First spring thing?
Mr Grigg always brings me home the first primrose of spring, just like my dear old dad used to do for my mother.

Favourite flower?
Wallflowers. Their scent takes me back to growing up in Somerset in the 1960s.

Favourite film?
The Jungle Book. I know all the words.

Care to share some wisdom?
There's no such word as can't (my primary school teacher)
Life is not a dress rehearsal (Mr Grigg)
Never turn down an invitation (Mrs Bancroft)
Just do it (Nike)

Now just a minute, you pompous old windbag...
(Winifred, the wife of Colonel Hathi, the elephant in *The Jungle Book*)

The only original piece of advice I can offer is: *if you ever feel intimidated by someone, imagine them naked.* Of course, this won't work if it's Elle Mcpherson or Posh Totty.

27 January: I wake to a load of crashing and the feeling I am being strangled. The throttling is The Medea Necklace which I have now been wearing for almost ten days because I am unable to get it off.

The noise is downstairs.

Mr Grigg leaps out of bed like Sher Khan the Tiger with a flaming branch attached to his tail. Something is going on. I look out from the window but there is no-one at the door. There is just a *tap-tap-tapping* and it's coming from our front room.

Naked, Mr Grigg tiptoes down the stairs, with me close behind. He thrusts open the door. Two beady eyes gaze at him. Mr Grigg glares back. A raven is sitting on the radiator, like a solitary note on a sheet of music.

They square up and do a little dance around the room, not taking their eyes off each other. Mr Grigg goes for the window, undoes the latch and throws it open. The raven looks one way and then the other. Should it fly out the window, risking the wrath of Grigg or back up the chimney?

It doesn't take long.

It makes a break for the window, looking over its shoulder as it shoots past Mr Grigg. I swear I hear it mutter *Nevermore* as it takes off into the great outdoors.

The excitement is too much.

Mr Grigg is angry.

'Can't even outwit a bloody raven,' he says. 'I've got to do something about my weight.'

It's not something that has ever bothered him before.

Chapter 2

February

1 February: I am in Waterstones looking at all the chick-lit rubbish on the shelves. In a fit of pique, I turn most of them round so they are facing the wrong way. I bet most of the authors slept with their publishers. If only I could be paid to write. But I've had yet another rejection letter for a feature article I wrote about island hopping in Greece.

And to top it all, Mr Grigg said to me yesterday: 'Will there be a point when you'll say "I'm not doing this anymore, I'm obviously not very good at it."? After all, you *are* nearly fifty.'

Tell that to the woman who wrote *Lark Rise to Candleford*. She was in her sixties when the first part of the trilogy was published. And I've just found out that Umberto Eco was forty nine when he wrote his first novel, *The Name of the Rose.*

There's hope for me yet.

2 February: Mr Grigg might have a point though. The freelance writing's not paying the bills so I am doing some admin work at the local council headquarters. I call it The Death Star. I feel like a battery hen. I do so miss my rural idyll.

Simple things like taking the dogs out in the morning light rather than stumbling around the fields as I fall over leads before the sun comes up. Hearing a robin warbling in the tree as I chat to neighbours in the street.

For three days a week, after donning my Marks & Spencer office 'uniform' of black, easy care trousers and a sensible sweater (with a brightly coloured top peeking out just to show I am a quiet rebel), I will get in my car and head for the office, some forty minutes away. I will listen inanely to Radio Two, flick over to more serious stuff on Radio Four and then get fed up with the line of questioning and mealy-mouthed responses. I will try Radio Local because the jingles always make me laugh. And then I will venture into Radio One territory but will get out quick in case I have a crash and the paramedics wonder who the hell this forty-eight- year-old thinks she is, listening to such rubbish. At least I am wearing clean and matching underwear. But not a thong. I am too old for a thong. I think Posh Totty wears a thong. Maybe I should try one.

Anyway, once I get to my destination, I will be unable to find anywhere to park and will drive around and around until I am almost back home.

I will finally find a space outside someone's house in a side street, clip-clop into town in the most ridiculous boots I have never worn, forge ahead across the zebra crossings and walk into the office. And along the cold corridors, other battery hens will be heading for their bunkers, doors closing as they reach their daily sanctuary, emerging like Pavlov's dogs every time the tea trolley bell rings.

I will open the door but no-one will look up. Instantly, I will feel guilty for arriving ten minutes after eight-thirty, even though I am a freelance and do not have to clock in. I will begin some incoherent ramble about being stuck behind a tractor and babble on for ages trying to justify myself before I will realise no-one is taking the slightest bit of notice. I will take off my invisibility cloak, put it on the back of my chair and log in. And still be invisible.

How I long to hear Russell's Crow cock-a-doodle-doo-ing across the valley.

3 February: Thank goodness for the book of witchcraft and practical magic I had for Christmas. The snow spell worked a treat. We're snowed in.

4 February: We are tucking into warm pancakes and Nutella in the kitchen of Pelly Sheepwash (*She Moves In Her Own Way*) after a brisk walk. Mr Loggins (*Night Boat to Cairo,* remember?) blows on his hands to warm them, and then, under the table, gives his wife, Darling (*I am What I Am*), a quick squeeze on the thigh.

Today's snow turns the village into a Bruegel painting. The primary school is closed and so is the comprehensive in the town over the hill. The village fields are full of children making snowmen, sledging, snowboarding and even skiing. Huge snow balls like the statues from Easter Island litter the hillside. The land echoes to the sound of excited shrieks and laughter.

'It's like Hampstead Heath up there,' says Pelly, as she helps me unravel The Medea Necklace, 'but without the lewd goings on.'

The nymph is wearing a hat of white snow and Celebrity Farmer announces on Facebook that he has opened up twenty one pistes but has no ski-lift. While everyone I speak to loves this weather because it means we're snowed in and a Blitz-like spirit wraps around this community like a never-ending scarf, animals still need feeding, farmers still need to work. It is a joy, then, to see Mamma Mia's husband walking with his trusty spaniel by his side. A retired farmer, he smiles and says quietly: 'I've been waiting for this for twenty years. To be able to go out in the snow and actually enjoy it because I'm not working.'

The last I saw of him, he walked off into a blizzard. He could be gone for some time.

5 February: The snow is melting but, hey, as I write, big dollops are coming down in Lush Places square. A severe weather warning has been issued for the South West over the next twenty four hours and with both of us working from home tomorrow, we are hoping for another snow day. It's looking good.

The Sheepwash family, like a gaggle of Von Trapps, have been up on the hillside snowboarding. Pelly and Mr Sheepwash were spotted zooming down the slopes - they call it 'Greys on Trays'.

Pelly is the steadiest person I know. Highly principled, with a Queen's Guide badge in common sense and parenting. She is the original earth mother, with four grown-up and scarily intelligent children. She bakes for England and makes the most wonderful vegetarian cuisine you have ever tasted.

Even that old Tory Mr Grigg has a soft spot for this leftie and her red beans and rice. But not too attracted, I hope. I think I need to talk to her.

6 February: I should be more trusting of that big man who is my husband. But there is always a part of me which is never quite sure. Just lately, he's had a certain swing in his swaggering step and I don't like it. Not a bit.

10 February: The great February Storm Moon greeted me as I took the dogs out just after dawn this morning. The patchwork square fields were lined with white all around the edges. You couldn't see the top of the hill for fog. The roads were awash with water and on my way into the Death Star I saw a car submerged under a bridge.

Celebrity Farmer has been moving dung all through the village. Mr Loggins has been using udder cream for his chapped hands. There has been no word of Mr St John. During the snow days, we could tell he was elsewhere because there were no tracks to and from his door.

Posh Totty has been flitting backwards and forwards in her white Land Rover Discovery to de-ice the horse trough. Even in her old clothes she's bloody attractive.

13 February: It is Valentine's Day tomorrow. I was in a card shop yesterday when a young lady said to the assistant: 'I know it's against the spirit of the thing, but do you sell Valentine's cards in multi-packs?' I could see her point. When you're that age, why put all your bets on one horse?

It reminded me that from about the ages of five to ten, I used to receive a card every year. I realise now my mystery admirer was my aunt who lived next door. But when I got to secondary school age and I didn't get one I was really upset. Then when I was twelve, I got sent a big padded card with a donkey on the front. It was from a genuine admirer, who missed a 'd' off my name and made me 'Madie'. I was so embarrassed, I hid it in a drawer because I was worried my mother would find it. She's a stickler for spelling and grammar.

I'm not very romantic. Bit of a cold fish really. I used to get a bit tearful at the J R Hartley advert for Yellow Pages, although I always smiled at the way he pronounced 'old' as 'ode' in the line: 'It is rather old' as if he came from Bridport. I'm sure the people who live there think *The Da Vinci Code* is about a very clever and artistic strain of influenza. However, Mr Grigg, despite his gruff exterior, is a great big softy. Lately, he's been buying me the slushiest cards he can find, with huge lettering on the front: 'To my wonderful wife' and then some naff poem inside. I'm touched, but he knows it makes me feel a bit weird, like rubbing cotton wool between my fingers. Yeuch. It also feels a bit false, as if he is trying to make up for something.

14 February: I cannot believe that Mr Grigg has taken me out for the evening to my home town, a place which smells of cottage pie and testosterone. You only had to look at someone in a funny way at my school and you'd get your face kicked in. And of all the places in the world to go for Valentine's night, Mr Grigg brings me here. It was meant to be a surprise. But the look on my face is the same as the one when we took the children on a canal barge holiday when they thought they were going to Alton Towers for a week.

We get to the Portuguese restaurant half-an-hour before it closes at seven o'clock. There are only two dishes left. It is unlicensed so we have no wine to wash down the food. The meal costs approximately £6. We adjourn to the pub next door, the one that was rebuilt after it caught fire during a drugs bust, and it is 'buy-one-get-one-free hour'. A girl with tattoos and a bleached blonde mother sit on a bar stool next to me. She says very loudly she feels like *kicking someone's fucking head in*. We leave.

Outside, Mr Grigg presents me with a boxed rose he picks up from the gutter. We drive on to a pub on the outskirts and gate-crash a party hosted by someone I was at school with. I meet the school bully who insists on hugging me and the hairs on my neck are rising. I feel like a nervous dog which has just been cornered. I am then introduced to a bald man who turns out to be the person to whom I lost my virginity in the fourth year.

For my Valentine's gift, Mr Grigg gives me a long handled wooden spoon and a pair of nutcrackers. And they say romance is dead. Bring on the slushy cards, for Christ's sake.

17 February: I am listening to *I Think I Love You* by David Cassidy. My mind drifts. I can see myself sitting at a desk in an open plan office, trying to type up a boring report being dictated to me through my headphones. The blank computer screen blinks. A door opens and a distinguished-looking man of about forty-something cuts a dash in a pin-striped suit. He sashays through and, in slow motion, he runs his fingers through his silver-tinged hair, pulls in his stomach and smiles at all the girls in the typing pool. He looks at me and winks and then trips over a power cable. He recovers himself expertly, brushes down his suit and walks on. I smile. I think I love him.

I'm in the back of a car, my face poking up through the sunroof like a ship's figurehead. It's dark, we're in a forest and no-one can hear my screams of absolute joy.

I fast forward to illicit meetings in a country pub, focus in on a newspaper with various adverts in the houses for rent section ringed round in red.

The film speeds up now. Angry, faceless partners, crockery thrown, children crying. And then moving into a new home. Comfortable domesticity, cooking together, flour on my nose, children growing up, tentatively holding each other's hands. Confrontations, children slamming doors, the two of us taking sides, feeling defensive, slamming doors and then making up. Possessiveness and jealousy.

And now we're here. Mr and Mrs Grigg. A Farrow and Ball purple front door with a dormant passion flower outside desperate to burst into bloom.

21 February: The strains of Bob Dylan filter up through the floorboards. I was having a lie-in until I woke to the sound of an iPod played very loudly through external stereo speakers. As I descend the staircase, Bob's nasal tones and constant beat of *Thunder on the Mountain* get louder.

I push the door open to find Mr Grigg in baggy tracksuit bottoms and nothing else, powering himself up and down on the stepper machine I bought him for Christmas. Sweat is pouring off his brow. It runs down his nose, hits his chin and then slams like a waterfall on his chest before trickling down his stomach.

He is oblivious to everything and sings along to Bob. I turn around and go back upstairs, knowing this is another of his get-fit-quick schemes. The sound of Bob could well be the soundtrack to the year.

Chapter 3

March

8 March: On a small hill above The Enchanted Village, Mr Loggins is busy dismantling the Love Shack. He and Darling Loggins have lived in this flimsy bungalow for two years, in wind and rain, in cold and icy weather with only their dream of opening a sustainable B&B keeping them alive.

There is a 360-degree view from here. You can literally see for miles and miles. To the tree-clad summit of Bluebell Hill, the BBC World Service masts standing out like giants and inland across fields towards Somerset.

It is cold up on the Love Shack roof and Mr Loggins is singing a locally-written song to keep himself warm:

Dorset is a'beautiful, wherever you go
And the rain in the summer-time makes the wurzle tree grow
When you're sitting in the spring-time in the thunder and the hail
With your true love, on a turnip stump, to hear the sweet nightingale

It is sunny down in the village but even the bronze nymph is wearing a poncho and Mr St John is in long trousers. So imagine how cold Mr Loggins must be up on that roof.

Now they have planning permission to build a new home, Mr Loggins is pulling the Love Shack apart. It is made of wood and corrugated iron. A hobbit hole in The Shire would have been more comfortable.

11 March: I've just been for a walk around Lush Places, courtesy of Google Street View. Mrs Bancroft is watching while a workman is rubbing down a piece of furniture outside her garage, Mr Champagne-Charlie has a female visitor on his doorstep and a man is walking a Lassie dog past our house.

A van is parked where it shouldn't be and Mamma Mia's husband, who has 'given up smoking', is sitting in the driver's seat and having a crafty fag, Mr Loggins is walking around the grounds of the Love Shack. The pub is shut and two people are getting out of their cars outside the village hall, which is bedecked with bunting.

It's a weird experience, and I don't like it much. Places caught in time, for people to peer into every nook and cranny.

Pelly Sheepwash will be pleased to know you can't see her lane. The Sheepwashlets could be up to all sorts of mischief and no-one would know. Quite right too. I zoom into my window but can't see myself looking out. That would be a paradox.

I scroll out to the Nether Regions of Lush Places and walk the little yellow peg man along a quiet green lane. I smile in recognition as I see Mr Grigg's Freeloader. And then I pan out. I suddenly feel very cold. His car is nose-to-nose with a white Land Rover Discovery.

12 March: Mr Grigg comes back from one of his regular jaunts to the tip. 'It's what men do, baby,' he tells me. He is dressed rather fetchingly in double denim and has a rather nasty looking red mark on his neck.

'What's that? I prod. It looks a bit suspect to me. Once upon a time, he was Hoss to my *Bonanza* and Trampas to my *Virginian*. But not any more. Not at the moment, at any rate.

'A horse bite,' he tells me, after much cajoling.

'A horse bite? At the tip? Mmm, I think they shoot horses, don't they? Why would anyone want to dump one?'

He refuses to be drawn. Bastard.

16 March: I have put my Google street view discovery and Mr Grigg's 'horse bite' to the back of my mind. Sometimes it pays to stick your head in the sand. I tell myself life's too short to worry. So I plaster over my doubt and get on with life. But I know this thing will niggle away at me. It will be the spider in the corner of the room that scuttles under the sofa. I will know it's still there.

But today, the sun streams through our bedroom window as if we are on holiday. Children's voices echo across the green, a Doppler-effect loud and then not-so-loud as two girls go up and down on the swings. A wood pigeon coos and a jackdaw rat-a-tat-tats. Mr Sheepwash flip-flops past with *The Observer*, the people up the road have their noses stuck in *The Sunday Telegraph* and a man from the council houses is wrapped up in the *News of the World*.

But this is very much *Mail on Sunday* territory, as the Tory posters that will soon stand proud in gardens and on windows in the lead-up to the elections will testify. Pelly once inadvertently picked up a note from the shop with her *Observer*, detailing a list of people in the village and the newspaper they read. There were no real surprises. I was half hoping Posh Totty took the

Sunday Sport, the new (female) vicar took *Playgirl* and the reactionary old colonel bought *Hello* magazine.

But they were virtually all *Daily Mail* readers.

22 March: It feels like the first morning of spring. The sky is clear and blue, the sun is glinting on the golden stone walls of the garden and the church bells are ringing. But this is Lush Places, the enchanted village where the man on number three bell is like Jonesy from *Dad's Army* and always several beats behind everyone else.

This morning, Mr Grigg throws the bedroom window open to let the day in. The songbirds are going full pelt, the jackdaws are cawing as they prepare themselves for bedding down in a suitable chimney when the time comes to nest. But if they think they're coming down ours they can think again. Nevermore.

A dove coos from the rooftops as the village folk amble to the shop across the square for their papers, narrowly missing the ginger wig scuttling up the road. A motorcycle chugs by, with that reassuring, low bubbling throaty sound only British bikes make. In the distance we can hear the faint sound of drum and bass from a boy racer's car going around the one-way system.

There is a clip-clip-clop and Mr Grigg gives an excited little wave.

It's that woman again.

March 23: Yesterday, I was in Hugh Fearnley-Whittingstall's canteen in Axminster. Mr Grigg took me there for lunch. Guilty conscience, probably. There is the map of the south west on the back of the door inside the shop and as I gazed at it, I did a double take. Lush Places stands out as the centre of the universe, its five roads joining in a pentangle right outside my house. They say the ley lines cross here.

When we're speaking to each other, Mr Grigg and I often count our blessings at living here, surrounded by beautiful countryside and good friends. In good weather and bad, even in the mist that swirls up around this high village perhaps a little too often, this is truly the lushest of places. When I die I want my ashes to be scattered on Bluebell Hill, with its beech trees, bluebells, toadstools and a view out onto the vale below and the sparkling sea beyond. It's such a beautiful, inspiring part of the world.

26 March: A taxi pulls up outside, bringing our dear neighbour, back from the grand tour. Suitcase after suitcase emerges from the car. And then Mrs Bancroft, the Queen of Sheba, in a wisp of chiffon, climbs elegantly from the cab and into the street, giving us all a wave.

She is back from warmer climes as the mists roll back with the arrival of spring. The weather does not suit her so she has been sitting like a princess on a Roman balcony overlooking the Spanish Steps for the past two months.

It seems as if the whole village has turned out to say hello. She waves graciously, like the Queen.

31 March: Excuse me for gloating but Mr Grigg had a bad night last night. He was tossing and turning as if he were on a spit. This morning, at breakfast, he told me he'd been having a nightmare.

'This is going to sound really weird...' he said, as I slurped my tea. 'But I dreamed I had a Cornish pasty stuck up my bottom.'

There was an interlude while he mopped up the PG Tips I spat all over him.

'Do you want me to tell you more?' he said. 'Or do you want to finish your Weetabix?'

I needed to know what happened next.

Once the Weetabix was safely down my gullet, he said: 'Well, I went to the doctor's, and I was in this kind of medical centre common room and there were lots of other doctors there. My doctor saw me and asked me what was wrong. I was really embarrassed and I whispered to him about the pasty. "Oh, don't worry about that," the doctor said, in a loud voice, "I've had one of those up my own bottom for the past eighteen months".'

At this point, I was trying to get the jam out of the jar for my toast but Mr Grigg almost ended up wearing it.

'So I didn't hang around,' he went on. 'If he couldn't get his own out, what chance did I have? So I tried to get it out and it took ages. It really hurt. And do you know why it hurt so much?'

No, I didn't have a clue but I could imagine a pasty up the jacksy could be a tad painful, even in a dream.

Completely straight-faced, he said: 'Well, it was a Ginsters pasty, and they're rectangular.'

'Was this really a dream or were you just telling me a joke?' I said.

'No, no,' Mr Grigg said. 'I dreamt it, honestly.'

I'm not a Ginsters expert but I don't think their pasties are rectangular. I think that's a chicken and mushroom slice. I'm sure they're very nice but, in all honesty, after Mr Grigg's dream I don't think I will be trying one to find out. In this household, it could be tempting fate. But it's one way of keeping your pasty warm I suppose.

Breakfast over, I kissed Mr Grigg on the forehead, patted his bottom and went out in the garden to collapse in a heap.

Serves him right. Karma for the horse bite.

Chapter 4

April

4 April: I don't know what's wrong with me. Why don't I just come out with it and ask him? Why would he confess if he thinks I don't know anything?

Posh Totty trots past and I feel like going out the front door and re-enacting a famous suffragette moment just to make a point.

8 April: Mr Grigg returned yesterday from the boss-eyed doctor's after a 'little operation'. He's been thinking about it a lot, which just might explain the pasty dream.

He walked into the kitchen as if he were John Wayne and had just got off his horse. He had tousled hair and the top two buttons of his work shirt were undone. He was fetchingly wearing double denim (both jeans and shirt) and looked rather raffish, like the man in that old Golf GTi advert who lost all his money in Monte Carlo. He smiled. He was still intact.

I had been worried about him. Our doctor is notorious for keeping people waiting. You can be his first appointment of the day and he still manages to be running half an hour late. Mr Grigg had already flounced out of the waiting room a couple of weeks ago when it slowly dawned on him he would be there at least an hour before seeing the doctor. Although thinking back to the pasty dream, the doctor is clearly a very busy man.

Mr Grigg hates being kept waiting. He also hates needles. So those two things, together with having what is called a 'tag' removed from a rather intimate place, did not bode well.

A short while later he was summoned into the surgery.

The boss-eyed doctor asked Mr Grigg to drop his boxers. The doctor prepared the syringe, peering myopically at it as he did so. Mr Grigg bent down for the doc to administer the injection.

He then proceeded to get out an implement similar to that used for removing ticks from dogs and cats and, while talking about antiques and grandfather clocks, whipped off the offending tag.

Both Mr Grigg and I would like to thank the doctor for keeping a steady hand. I had visions of myself after the operation standing in front of a papal chair with Mr Grigg perched above the hole in its seat. I would do a 'grope the Pope' test from below, apparently a ritual deriving from the Pope Joan legend, to declare 'he has testicles'. Mr Grigg would then stand up and pontificate.

Fortunately for me (but not necessarily for Mr Grigg, who deserves to be manhandled, the way I'm feeling about him at the moment), this was not required.

April 14: The top of Bluebell Hill is completely obscured by fog and the ground is squelchy and damp underfoot. In the street, the recycling boxes and bags are full of paper, bottles and cans. The Grigg abode is no exception, with an extra bag for bottles after a party to welcome new neighbours, Mr and Mrs Putter. They've lived here for six months but we just hadn't got around to initiating them properly in village life. Sitting in our kitchen they were quite taken aback when the doorbell kept ringing. Villager after villager strolled through our front door, clutching wine bottles and cans and even bottles of champagne.

'This is for you, chap,' Mr Champagne-Charlie said, as he pressed a bottle of best Moet into Mr Grigg's chest, while Bubbles, his wife, hiccupped and giggled like a schoolgirl.

'Been on the sauce already, then, Bubbles?' Mr Grigg said. She giggled again and found a comfy chair to collapse in.

Posh Totty glided in with MDF Man, Nobby Odd-Job, the Logginses and Ted Moult and Jamie Lee.

And then a waft of perfume headed our way in the shape of the fragrant Mrs Putter.

'We didn't expect all these people', she said.

'Neither did we,' I replied.

Eighteen guests crammed into the our tiny house, enjoying Mr Grigg's stuffed rabbit and roasted vegetable tart, my bread and butter pudding made with Lidl's panettone and a pavlova I renamed 'effing mess' after dropping it on the floor. When Celebrity Farmer and Mr Champagne-Charlie drank us out of house and home, Mrs Bancroft was sent across the road to her house for reinforcements and came back clutching three bottles of white wine.

'They're not chilled,' she said, 'I just grabbed them from the cellar.'

I ask you. You just can't get the staff these days.

19 April: It has been a busy weekend. However, we managed to find time to go into the pub yesterday afternoon for a spot of drinking and driving in the form of Scalextrix Sunday. This is a new event in which fully grown men and women get to play around with electric cars. Children are, in the main, banned from taking part. This is probably because one of the best racers was a young lad called Jensen, aged about eleven, whose focus and determination was worthy of Jackie Stewart. Middle aged men were quaking in their trainers.

I was bemused when Dudley came in and requested a pint of water rather than his usual distinctive tipple – Grand Marnier. He looked rather dashing in a Toulouse Lautrec-style beret and cane. At least, I think he had a cane, but perhaps I imagined that. It transpired the beret was not just for effect - it was hiding five stitches. On Saturday, a little worse for wear, Dudley went outside for a smoke, leaned over to put his fag out in the receptacle provided but just carried on leaning. It was a fag too far and he ended up banging his head on the cobbles.

I do hope we will see him out again. A week or so ago, we went in to the pub for a romantic dinner for two. When I asked for some background music, before Larry the Landlord had a chance to put on the Chi-Lites Greatest Hits (quite a small CD) or say 'shall I sing *New York New York*?', Dudley came out from Compost Corner – where the regulars sit at the end of the bar - perched on the piano stool and started to play, serenading us with *As Time Goes By* and other such tunes. A couple on the next table who were celebrating their wedding anniversary looked up and said: 'Oh, isn't this lovely?'

Mr Grigg and I wish Dudley well. We are rather fond of him. His fall could have happened to any of us. He's not the first person to have injured himself in this way. And he certainly won't be the last.

20 April: The red wine in our pub is the kind you wouldn't take to someone's for supper even if you disliked them.

A large glass and a small glass of dreadful red wine later, the bar thins out to about eight of us. Larry the landlord puts on a *Sound of Music* CD given to him by the local bus driver who got it free with the *Daily Mail*. As the strains of *Climb Every Mountain* permeate the pub, the assembled throng begin to sing.

In fine voice is Hawkeye, a 60-year-old steel erector whose Dorset drawl is like a West Country version of John Wayne. As the introduction to *Do-re-mi* tinkles in, I am seven again and at the primary school social, but this time taking the leading role. Without thinking, I become Maria, finger pointing, and directing the locals sitting on stools at the bar into their parts like seven restless children. Some of them are reluctant, it's true, and Mr St John's '*So, a needle pulling thread*' is a bit weak but Hawkeye's '*La, a note to follow So*' is positively breathtaking. And Dudley's '*Tea, a drink with jam and bread*' is just angelic.

It is one of the best bits of improvised singing I have heard in the pub for ages, with Caruso, a professional singer, bringing us all back to '*Do*' again.

Now we are on a high, the landlord takes this as his cue for a bit of Larry-oke. As the opening bars of *Dancing Queen* break through, Pelly Sheepwash, Darling Loggins, Mrs Bancroft and I take to the microphones and become Meryl Streep et al for the evening.

It's enough to wake the neighbours.

But we *are* the neighbours, so it's all right.

23 April: It's St George's Day and up on the hill, Mr Loggins is bashing down the Love Shack until only a Parthenon gable remains.

'Someone's coming to take the windle,' he says. I think he means window. He says 'chimbley' in the next sentence.

Well, he *is* from Bridport.

24 April: The sun is bathing the enchanted village of Lush Places in bright light and glorious heat.

I drop off Number One Son at the railway station with a snowboard the length of the Panama Canal under his arm. Cruising home in the Freeloader, driving through country lanes to avoid the main road and its stationary cars, The Mamas and the Papas are singing *'It's getting' bedder...'* while I do accompanying yelling on harmonies.

A large grey Land Rover Discovery approaches but doesn't appear to be slowing down. The driver seems to be an upper class twit in a flat cap.

We edge past each other in the narrowest part of the lane. We are just about to do synchronised growling through open windows when I realise it's Mr Champagne-Charlie.

'I didn't think you were going to stop,' he says.

'I didn't think you were either,' I say. 'I thought you were...'

Bubbles' voice pipes up from the passenger seat: 'An ass in a hat?'

Not only my next-door neighbour but telepathic too.

I drive on to the top of Loggins Lane, where the Love Shack used to be. The only thing left now is a solitary chimney and fireplace, a monolith surrounded by wasteland, with one of the best views in Dorset. Mr Loggins has been busy.

A 'proper', old-style Land Rover chugs up the hill. I come to a halt and as the driver passes and he waves like the Queen to thank me for stopping. It's Celebrity

Farmer in his 'day' vehicle as opposed to his special-occasion-Porsche.

Around the corner, Nobby Odd-Job's Range Rover gleams as it stands in his driveway.

Four four by fours.

But no sign of a white one.

26 April: It is late in the evening and from my window I catch a glimpse of a shadow skulking around the square. It is attached by a thin line to the shadow of a dog. Not long after, Mr Champagne-Charlie and his dog, Wiggy, appear.

But it's no ordinary dog walk tonight. He ties Wiggy up to the bin outside the shop and then pulls out a shotgun.

He eyes up his target, warily, and then edges along the wall of the village green, SAS-style. It's a bit like watching Edward Woodward as *Callan*. He takes a quick look around him before taking aim and firing.

PING.

The replaced streetlight outside the house suddenly goes out. Mr Champagne-Charlie puts the gun away in its case over his shoulder, goes back to Wiggy, pats her on the head and walks off up the one-way system.

He doffs his cap, theatrically, in my direction as he sees me looking out of the window.

27 April: A young man in a suit supervises the children in their pretty dresses and best trousers. They screech around the village green, jumping on and off swings, rattling through the play fort and whizzing down the slide. The bells ring out across the square and the sun beats down as people go to the shop for their papers and lottery tickets while guests in their glad rags get out from their cars to go to church.

A village wedding, and everyone has a spring in their step.

Super Mario paints the outside of the shop, where the 'for sale' sign hangs ominously on the corner. Mr Grigg and Mr Loggins drive by with Nobby Odd-Job's trailer, fetching bits of wood from the Love Shack demolition site. At the village pump, Larry the Landlord gossips with record producer Ding Dong Daddy, whose arms flail around wildly as if he is an orchestra conductor.

'Did you hear that noise last night?' I think Ding Dong Daddy is saying. 'It sounded like a gun going off.'

'Didn't hear a thing, mate,' I imagine Larry is saying. 'We had karaoke on all night. You should have been there, you'd have loved it. We had Mr Champagne-Charlie singing Barry White and Posh Totty shimmying to Santana. Cracking, it was.'

I bristle at the thought.

During the day, several other people mention the sound of gunfire. Nervously, I finger The Medea Necklace (it's become a permanent fixture as I still can't get it off) as I feign surprise. I'm all for direct action to get rid of these hideous street lights no-one in the village asked for but it pays to keep quiet.

This evening, I find two freshly-gutted rabbits in a bag on the doorstep. Payment for my silence. Just right for supper. Someone's been busy.

28 April: It's election time and the West Dorset countryside is awash with huge blue posters for our incumbent Tory MP, Oliver Letwin. Here and there, you see the odd splash of orange - a quiet, polite hoorah for the Liberal Democrats - but nothing at all for the others. I don't even know who our Labour candidate is.

I'm aware, though, that our local Green Party candidate is a very gentle-looking Mrs Greene from Sherborne, who will probably get my vote for having the surname most like its owner.

Politics is a personal thing. In the Grigg household, we don't talk about it much, as Mr Grigg and I sit on opposite sides of the fence, waiting for it to topple over.

He has never forgiven an old flatmate who completely ruined his Edward Du Cann sign by altering the second and last letters in *Cann* and then sticking the poster in the window. Mr Grigg was nearly done for obscenity.

Over the years, there has been some inspired defacing of political signs. Oliver Letwin became *LetwinD* and outside the railway station, just over the border into Somerset, I see the Tory candidate's features have been cut out to make him totally faceless.

In a nearby village, I saw two signs for what I thought were the Lib-Dems, only to find they were advertising llamas.

At supper last night, politics reared its ugly head when Nobby Odd-Job, a retired policeman, announced he was conducting an investigation.

It appears one of the guests had defaced an election leaflet in his study, giving that nice Mr LetwinD horns, spectacles and a twirly moustache.

'That's sedition,' he said, sending Mrs Bancroft and me running to a dictionary to look it up.

'I have eliminated several suspects,' Nobby said, glaring at me intently.

Of course, I denied everything. What ever happened to innocent until proved guilty?

This morning, I receive an email:

Lengthy investigations reveal:

'The WRITER with the PEN in the STUDY' to be the main suspect'

A minute later, the UKIP battle van pulls up outside my house, with flags a-waving and loudspeaker a-hailing.

While the driver goes to the shop for his *Daily Mail,* I am half tempted to stick a banana up the van's exhaust pipe. But I think better of it. Would I get legal aid for a charge of sedition? Probably not.

29 April: Bugger me, that nice Mr LetwinD has only just come and knocked on my door, asking for my vote. Does he not *know* I've been *accused of sedition* by one of his most ardent supporters in Lush Places?

'Hello, I'm Oliver Letwin,' he says.

And I nearly say 'Yes, I know, although you look different without the horns, moustache and specs.'

But I don't. Obviously.

'Can I count on your vote?'

'Well, at least one half of the household.'

'Your husband? Are you wavering?'

'You could say that,' I say, thinking he can probably see my Young Socialist past just by looking at my face. So I blurt out: 'I think you're a great constituency MP' as if I've got George Clooney on the doorstep.

Mr LetwinD smiles sweetly. He is a very nice man, even if he did write the Conservative Party manifesto.

I shuffle, we both look embarrassed, the clock strikes thirteen and the ginger wig, which I have not seen for some time, blows past. Just as I wonder what to say, the frozen-moment chasm is filled by the UKIP ice cream van going by, flags-a-waving, a military march-a-blaring.

Saved by the bell.

30 April: I don't believe it. Me, a one-time-almost-hunt-saboteur as a teenager, in the sponsors' area at the annual point-to-point races. We have a stunning view of the racetrack, the paddock and it's just a short stroll to the bookies' stands.

I am not quite sure how I managed to get into this ringside position, with the hampers and champers, picnics and shooting sticks. The toffs' trousers - red and calf-scour yellow - the *Dubarry* boots and the ties and pullovers. It's not what you know, it's who you know, and with Mr and Mrs Champagne-Charlie as chaperones, no-one bats an eyelid.

The point-to-point, you see, is run by the local hunt. I am a rural child but I am not a hunt fan, although my views have mellowed over the years, partly in reaction to an urban government imposing its will on its country cousins. So I justify my attendance as an observer, aided by my camera and notebook rather than aniseed spray.

On the first race, I place a very small bet on *Tell All*, a feisty little creature, while Mr Grigg put his money on *Wilde Thing*, a horse so laid back it could be a deckchair. The odds on Number Eleven go up as an attractive, black stable-lass helps lead the horse around the paddock.

'Oooh, I'm backing thic one there,' choruses a group of Young Farmers, wearing sweatshirts carrying various double entendre about squirrels, nuts and bushes.

Classy.

Tell All runs out at the first fence, last seen nine miles down the road at Axminster. Wilde Thing comes in third, Mr Champagne-Charlie's horse, *Twiggie*, is still putting on the wrinkle cream in the M&S changing room, and his wife's steed, also backed by Mrs Bancroft, comes in first. The ladies are just raking it in.

A long refrain of what sounds like a horse breaking wind comes over the public address system, followed by a hectoring rant by the commentator to get the punters to vote Tory on May 6. A child locks himself in a four-by-four and plays a very noisy tune on the vehicle's horn while mummy, daddy, grandma and grandpa sit braying around the picnic table, drunk and oblivious.

The horses are wearing Boden under their saddles and the final race is sponsored by a firm of funeral directors.

At the end of it all, Mrs Bancroft and Mrs Champagne-Charlie are £20 in pocket. Both Mr Grigg and Mr Champagne-Charlie have had two respectable wins. And me? Nothing. Not a bean. Too busy looking at everything else around me when I should have been studying form.

Through the champagne haze, a poster on the other side of the race circuit has been puzzling me:

'Sexhausts and shocks'

and then a number advertising a twenty four hour service.

In a moment of revelation, I suddenly see another word at the beginning of the sentence. It now reads: 'Brakes exhausts and shocks' and is advertising a local garage. A comma – or lack of it – can make such a difference.

And then I see Mr Grigg, in animated conversation with Posh Totty, bedecked in *Barbour* and *Boden*. I finger The Medea Necklace, which feels like a thin boa constrictor.

Chapter 5

May

1 May: I walk up to the cricket pitch, past the wild honesty, dead nettles and red campions.

From the roadside I can make out Mr Grigg yelling at Mr Sheepwash to run faster as that turncoat Loggins bats for the other side. I hear leather on willow, closely followed by 'clunk' as a ball whizzes over the top of the hedge and on to a passing car. The elderly occupants duck when the blow strikes but drive on. They look terrified. They probably think they have strayed into a parallel universe (which would be correct) and hit by molten lava from *Dantes Peak* or caught in the *Millennium Falcon* as it storms through the asteroid belt.

2 May: Today I heard the unmistakable voice of the cuckoo. Her call has not been heard here for years. It makes me smile.

The cuckoo flowers are washing the fields with drifts of pink, the bluebells are coming out on the banks and in the woods. And the swallows and house martins dart in and out of the square, chattering as they go. A pair of Brent geese flap by, pointing out places of interest along the way.

All we are waiting for is the ceremonial unveiling of the bronze nymph. Then we will know summer is just around the corner.

3 May: War has been declared in the village, where political posters have replicated like Mickey Mouse's broom in *The Sorcerer's Apprentice*.

Unlike the urban wasteland of Bridport, in the rural hinterland we have seen tit-for-tat explosions of blue and orange. Luckily for those who worry about rural aesthetics, these are complimentary colours.

In my household, Mr Grigg is now threatening to put up a poster for Mr LetwinD. So I am scrabbling around for a Labour poster in case he actually gets round to it. Although I might chicken out and put up an orange one for the Lib Dems. I might have to show political balance and put up a Green one as well, although I do draw the line at UKIP, however rousing their music.

By Thursday, my house could look like a beatnik's guitar case or a Mod's lapel. Stickers and badges everywhere.

It's amazing, though, because in the past, the people of Lush Places kept their political preferences to themselves. But for the first time, they're nailing their allegiances very publicly to the mast.

It usually happens when a large Oliver LetwinD placard appears in someone's garden. Overnight, a poster for the Lib Dem candidate, Sue Farrant, goes up next door.

People still smile sweetly to each other as they collect their respective *Daily Mails* and *Guardians* from the village shop. But there is an almost Gordon Brownish edge to their fixed grins.

'Bigot,' they mutter through gritted teeth.

We have had a steady stream of political candidates filing through, knocking on doors and posting missives through our letterbox. I had a letter from David Cameron last week, which was very good of him because he must be extremely busy. As well as having a visit from that nice MrD LetwinD, I've had callers from the Lib Dems and a woman I think was Mrs Greene from the Greens. Or Miss Scarlet from the Red Brigade.

In between times, the candidates have been dodging the UKIP ice cream van as it drives up and down the village.

It has all become rather exciting. And it's hotting up – we're hosting a party on election night, with guests chosen for their political persuasions.

As this would never have happened a few years ago, when to admit to *not* voting Tory in this village was akin to revealing you were HIV positive, I'm looking forward to it, although I could do with a few suggestions about what food I should put on.

Ah, yes. Revenge. A dish best served cold.

4 May: Anakin Sheepwash's birthday. May the fourth be with you.

The bronze nymph has disappeared. Her plinth is bare. We were all looking forward to seeing her nakedness again, like Botticelli's Venus rising from her slumber. Now only emptiness welcomes visitors.

It could be that she has been taken in for some routine maintenance. I fear, however, it might be propriety. Someone, somewhere, is fearful for our moral souls.

Because this morning, a very large people carrier dropped off a gaggle of Jehovah's Witnesses at the top of the village. They were sent forth in pairs in various directions. The ones at my door were very nice, giving me a leaflet and then asking me if it was OK to smell my wallflowers, which I thought perhaps might be code for 'this one's going to burn in hell'.

But their appearance made a change from all the political callers we've been having lately. I understand we are in what is now considered a marginal seat, made all the more marginal, I fear, by the Tories' own campaign posters urging people to Vote for Change. This is if a conversation Mr Loggins had with old people in Sherborne this week is anything to go by. He swears it is absolutely true, and it goes something like this:

'Hello ladies, and what do you think about this election then? Decided who you are going to vote for?'

'Well,' says one. 'We're a bit confused. We've been voting Conservative all our lives but now they're telling us we've got to vote for change. So we're thinking about voting Liberal Democrat. That Mr Clegg seems such a nice man.'

5 May: Tomorrow is election day in Lush Places and things are deadly quiet.

People wearing blue rosettes are stalking the village. I am invited in for coffee by my district councillor who tells me it doesn't matter what my politics are and do I take sugar.

I have sort of nailed my colours to the mast this time around, making a statement in a sea of blue. I am voting tactically, even if Gordon Brown says I shouldn't, because to do anything else around here would be a waste of a vote. So an orange poster now accompanies Mr Grigg's blue one in the front window. The colours look good against the purple door and profusion of wallflowers and pink and black tulips.

However, I have a sneaking admiration for the man up the road who has Labour posters all over his house and garden, in a village which is a sea of blue.

When I see him in the pub, I walk across the bar to congratulate him.

'I thought you were going to punch me,' he says, flinching.

Tomorrow night we are holding an election party, with our neighbours Mr and Mrs Champagne-Charlie, Mrs Bancroft and Nobby Odd-Job. I have persuaded my good friend Pelly Sheepwash and Anakin to attend, just to restore some political balance.

There is only so much Tory guffawing I can take. I also need allies. Nobby Odd-Job is conducting a second investigation after his Tory poster was removed from his garden.

Without wishing to protest too much, I can honestly say it was not me.

6 May: An old black dog cocks its leg up against the tulips next to the village pump. A woodpecker drills into a tree trunk down on the common. The dandelions stay firmly closed in the cold morning air.

Grey skies and drizzle in Lush Places. A perfect day for an election.

At the Grigg hovel today, attempts have been made to alter the names on our posters to read Sue *Farright* and Oliver *Leftwing*.

A few folks make their way up to the polling station, but things are pretty quiet. You could hear a hat-pin drop. Outside the door, a teller with a blue rosette chomps on an apple and asks for my number. She smiles a thank you and reveals a ghastly, gaping tunnel of masticated apple, edged with violent mauve lipstick seemingly applied by Bette Davies in *What Ever Happened to Baby Jane*.

There is a sign pointing the way in to the polling station but nothing to show you the way out. You can check in any time you like, but you can never leave.

Like something from *A Sound of Thunder*, a famous short story by Ray Bradbury and all about the butterfly effect, the scenery tomorrow could look very different, depending on what people do today. It's in our hands.

Tonight there are tensions as two televisions – one tuned to the BBC and the other to ITV – compete for attention in the front room and kitchen. Champagne-Charlie has on his best toffs' gear and is lording it over the widescreen and the BBC, along with the other Tories. Pelly, Anakin and I are sitting on the sofa in the kitchen, watching ITV, lower down in the house and pecking order but claiming the higher moral ground.
'Shall we play cards?' says Mr Sheepwash, as yet another Tory victory is announced.
'Yes, let's,' I say, even though I know I am not going to win against this card shark.
'How on earth can you vote for that Gordon Brown?' Champagne-Charlie says on his way to the kitchen for another drink. 'He's just so ugly.'
'Looks don't come into it,' Pelly says.
'Obviously not,' Champagne-Charlie says, quaffing back his third gin and tonic.
This could be a long night.

7 May: I'm a bit tired but our election here in West Dorset is over. Just to say that Mr Grigg is cock-a-hoop and working out on the stepper with great joy to *Thunder on the Mountain*. Mr LetwinD retained his seat. He's a very nice man, even if I didn't vote for him. I will let Mr Grigg have his moment of glory, just like he didn't allow me to have mine in 1997. But I don't forget easily.

Anyway, I'm taking the posters down from the window as I listen to Bob Dylan and the stepper machine and Mr Grigg going thump-thump-thump.

9 May: Despite the election, May is absolutely the best month, with the lime green leaves of trees on the village green and the gypsy lace, pink campions, bluebells and yellow dead nettles along the banks of the lanes. The fields are full of buttercups, dandelion clocks, cuckoo flowers and speedwell.

There are wallflowers in pots outside my front door, a huge sign on the playground fence advertising a fete tomorrow (complete with snail racing and paintballing) and the remains of some tulips next to the village pump. The latter is due for another revamp in the shape of concrete containers filled with bedding plants, courtesy of a villager who wants to brighten up the square. Good on her, but please God don't let her put begonias in. They make my flesh creep.

The tree pollen is making me sneeze. I've not always been a sneezer. I was born and brought up in the countryside where hay fever is for softies. But when I got into my thirties I started sneezing for England. It usually happens mid-morning or mid-afternoon and can be triggered by pollen, dust and perfume. And when I sneeze, I don't just sneeze once. No, I'll go on at least a dozen times and they'll be of superhero loudness. No cat-type or terrier sneeze for me, thank you very much.

11 May: It is strimming season in The Enchanted Village and with it comes the inevitable expletives from the Grigg garage. On lawns and in workshops all over the village, the strimmers suddenly take on lives of their own, like the broomsticks in Harry Potter. They even have names. Mr Sheepwash has three adjectives for his and one noun - bastard - as the starting-up the strimmer process turns into a little dance.

The smell of petrol and the sound of swear words fill the air, the engine floods and Pelly Sheepwash sagely shakes her head.

'They don't like stale petrol,' she whispers to me, adding that she told Mr Sheepwash this last summer. This has since been confirmed by the local agricultural engineer who says he is besieged by bastard strimmers in the spring when the men of the house reach the end of their tethers and can deal with the frustration no more.

'Well, my car starts when I leave it for a few days,' Mr Sheepwash says, rather snappily for one so usually laid back.

'Yes,' says Pelly. This woman has the patience of a saint. 'But you don't leave it in a shed all through the winter and just expect it get going as soon as you put your key in the ignition, do you?'

As Mr Sheepwash finally gets his strimmer going, Mr Grigg throws his (also called Bastard) down in disgust and then straps it to his bike for the ride home. This seemed like a good idea at the time but once he has started, he cannot stop and has to ride into the hedge to brake.

At that point, a John Wayne-style hiccup is heard from up the road. It is Hawkeye, who has been in the pub all afternoon and is at last winding his way home, his grey tracksuit bottoms making him look like Colonel Hathi from *The Jungle Book*.

'Sorry, I can't speak proper, I got hiccups.'

It's a strange old place.

13 May: I asked Mr Grigg today if he wouldn't mind taking me to the station tomorrow.

'Sorry sweetheart,' he said, 'I've got something else lined up.'

He wouldn't tell me what, despite me threatening to deprive him of sex over the next month. So we slept in separate rooms. This is a war of attrition.

14 May: The country mouse is off to town. Celebrity Farmer gives me a lift to the station on his tractor. It's not easy, balancing a small suitcase in the cab, especially as the world and his wife seem to think they should be waving at us. I stopped waving back when I almost lost the suitcase under the wheel arch.

I am off to London as I'm booked into a travel writing workshop at the ITV Studios in London under an assumed name. I have been looking forward to this for some time, as it is run by travel writer Rory Maclean, of *Magic Bus* and *Falling for Icarus* fame, and the *Guardian's* Dea Birkett. I heard Rory Maclean give a talk once. His gentle, Canadian tones sent me far away.

I have just found out who the guest editors are and I am working myself up to do a pitch. I'm not in the best frame of mind, considering my fall-out with Mr Grigg. I am also rubbish at selling myself so I hope my sparkling prose will speak for itself.

I am sitting on the train from Crewkerne to Waterloo and the world is whizzing past me. A man in a straw hat is painting at an easel in a field, a line of cows is walking across the meadow, country houses, thatch, trees, bushes, back gardens, smiling people cycling along country lanes.

I am excited. Very excited. I am listening on my iPod to my nephew and his rapping band, representing the west, with a pocketful of poems and high hopes. In the carriage around me, there is a young man with a little beard and glasses with a large rucksack wedged under the seat. An older woman is reading Rose Tremaine and a girl with a ring through her nose is flicking through her phone and smiling to herself.

A heavily pregnant woman sighs as a concerned husband fusses around her. An old man shakes his head and buries it back into *The Times*.

We stop at Yeovil Junction, Sherborne, Templecombe, Gillingham, Tisbury, Salisbury with its dreaming spire and then on to Basingstoke and then Woking where The Jam came from and Clapham Junction. Nearing our destination now, with its concrete greyness, tall buildings, plenty of cars but devoid of people on the streets. Every time I pass some of these flats I think of gritty police series on television and wonder how people can live here.

And then I glimpse The London Eye, Big Ben and the Houses of Parliament. It makes me reach for The Medea Necklace.

We've arrived. My big moment.

15 May: In the city, everything goes by so fast. Taxis, buses, cars and people. I hear strains of Latin American music from a café and decide to sit down for a coffee. Watching these people is fascinating as they flit from place to place on a giant hamster's wheel no-one can stop.

Even the clouds whizz by in extra quick time. And the hands of Big Ben seem to turn oh-so- quickly as the city shakes and wobbles and struts and wiggles and high kicks into life.

I have had a lovely night with an old friend with whom I trained as a journalist thirty years ago. She's a huge success now, head of communication for a major international company. I work in admin for the county council.

Underneath the clock at Waterloo Station, the gateway to my Western world, I look to see which platform my train will be on. I try ringing Mr Grigg but there is no-one at home.

I think about my pitch at the travel writing workshop. I'd been buoyed up by euphoria after being told by the trainer Dea Birkett that my notes in an exercise about using all the senses sounded like poetry. But when it came to pitching an idea to the editor of *Wanderlust*, my heart was knocking so hard against my chest I thought I might have to let it out and shake hands with everyone round the table.

Rather bravely, I went straight in with my first paragraph about the wind turbines in Puglia, *encircling me like a sinister army*, and then waved a collage of my photos for all to see. The editor was kind, said Puglia was a bit old hat but it was a nice opening paragraph. Dea ran her fingers through her boyish crop and screeched: 'Cut out all those adjectives', rang her bell and said: 'Next' My heart wanted to bounce down the table and punch her on the nose.

Afterwards, trudging along the South Bank with my little pink case, I wished Mr Grigg was there to hold my hand, carry my heavy bags and to tell me I was wonderful.

I give him a call on the mobile but it is switched through to answerphone.

At the station, a man with a guitar walks by, followed by a tall Chinese girl wearing a red silk shirt and cowboy boots, an old couple out for the day and a young black man in a pinstripe suit. People of all shapes and sizes, colours and races, sexes, in iPod bubbles, Moonwalk hats and medals, shuffling, walking, *Mind The Gap*, running, sneezing, the smell of unwashed hair, boots, sandals, trainers, deck shoes, escalator up, escalator down and all to the soundtrack of *Unfinished Sympathy* by Massive Attack on my iPod. I am fixed to the spot as the world of London dances around me.

I finally arrive home and Mr Grigg is not there.

18 May: I find myself on Bluebell Hill, overlooking The Enchanted Village, where the colours are so intense they are almost blinding. The bluebells here are known throughout Dorset. The woods are filled with heady aromas and a dazzling array of bright colours. It is a time when the ground and sky are wearing matching outfits in a deep and lovely, glorious blue.

The clean, lime green of the beech trees, the swathe of bluebells, an ocean of them, oh so blue. And then very occasionally, a white one pops up out of nowhere. This place is magical at the best of times and May *is* the best of times, even when, especially when, you're feeling fed up.

A hollow tree where a goblin sits, a fallen trunk inscribed with names going back fifteen years when university students were still at primary school, a couple sitting on a grassy bank, soaking up the sun and enjoying the view.

The patchwork fields, cosy hills and an undulating ridge underlining the millpond sea. I want the landscape to wrap me all up and make me feel safe, warm and secure. And wanted.

22 May: Hey, it's not a big deal. Not a big deal at all. But I'm a little bit excited because *The World from my Window* has been chosen as a Blog of Note by Google's

Blogger team. I only know that because my list of followers has suddenly shot up from about 50 to 500.

There are comments from people in Kentucky, Tennessee, Canada, Sydney and Pakistan.

I've gone global.

Put that in your pipe and smoke it, Dea Birkett.

24 May: Despite the Blog of Note accolade, no-one has beaten a path to my door. I thought I might have been invited to put something in for the Booker, or at least the Bridport Prize. But the brass knocker on the Farrow and Ball door has become home to a massive spider's web.

Meanwhile, Bob Dylan's *Thunder on the Mountain* is thumping up through the floorboards as Mr Grigg continues his punishing exercise schedule.

'I've got to get my weight down,' he says. But why? I like him as he is.

26 May: My friend, Tuppence, is a slip of a thing. She looks about twelve but is obviously older because she has two grown-up children. Her asymmetrical bob is whizzing from side to side as she takes us through our paces in the village hall.

We are standing there, in lines, as the Latin beats get us moving, shimmying, shuffling, whooping and hollering.

'No shirking at the back!' Tuppence yells.

I turn around, the fragrant Mrs Putter to my right and Pelly Sheepwash to my left. Along the back row are Mr Champagne-Charlie, Mr Grigg and Mr Loggins, doing their best to keep up at this dance taster session but obviously only there to leer at the wiggling bottoms of the women in front of them.

And, inevitably, bang in front of Mr Grigg is Posh Totty.

I might have known.

Bastard.

27 May: Last night we slept in separate rooms again. I woke up this morning and couldn't remember why I was in a different bed. I vaguely remember knocking back the bad white wine in the pub and arguing with Mr Grigg once we got home. But I have no idea what it was about. And I'm not asking him what it was about, either.

Bastard.

28 May: Tonight, a big old Dyad Moon is suspended low in the sky. It is a deep rusty orange, with wisps of clouds like chiffon around its neck. It is nearly midnight in The Enchanted Village and there is a constant, low hum - the sound of British motorbikes trundling through on a late night Whitsun bank holiday rally.

Down the road, the lane to Bluebill Hill is strewn with homemade patchwork bunting, hung between the lilac trees, May blossom hedges and Narnia lamp posts. Tomorrow, there is to be a wedding in Lush Places and a sneak preview of the marriage venue promises something akin to when Jane Austen met Thomas Hardy.

And still the British bikes hum through The Enchanted Village, as the wedding guests snuggle down into unfamiliar beds and the bride tries to get to sleep after a Baileys or two, remembering that this time tomorrow she will have a completely different name, a completely different life.

And three hundred and fifty years ago tomorrow, on Oak Apple Day, King Charles II was restored to the

English throne. An auspicious date for a wedding between a monarchist and his republican-bride-to-be. But take heart, the Dyad Moon signifies complementary colours, left and right, a two-ness coming together as one.

31 May: Pelly's daughter, her Number One Sheepwashlet, married her soulmate in the wonderful setting of Forde Abbey, which nestles inside the Dorset border, with just a nod to neighbouring Somerset for its postal address.

There were gasps when the bride walked in with Mr Sheepwash to a score composed by the *Cinematic Orchestra*, as the huge log fire blazed in the great hall. A Jane Austen heroine, she took the arm of her husband-to-be, who in the film of this book will be played by a young Hugh Grant or maybe Dominic Cooper. There was even a distinguished wedding guest in a kilt. And the assembled throng sniggered when the registrar asked the bridegroom to repeat the words: 'I Timothy St John Dauphinoise Sutherland...'

The guests gathered below the abbot's lodgings and tower (built by the last abbot, Thomas Chard, in the early sixteenth century) for a group photo as the female photographer tried to conduct the proceedings while balanced precariously on the parapet.

There were hats and frocks and shoes, champagne flutes, bridal bouquets of sweet peas and floral arrangements of blousy peonies and sumptuous lilac, a jazz band playing in the orangery, a fountain like Old Faithful on the far side of the croquet lawn and some fine English drizzle.

And Mr Grigg even gave my hand a squeeze and told me he loved me. A romantic setting and a few glasses of bubbly works wonders.

Today, the sun beats down for the picnic on Bluebell Hill as Mr Grigg ferries the less able and two beer barrels to the top. Some fifty people sit on blankets and chairs and to hell with the National Trust as the children play Frisbee and football in among the beech trees. There is Italian bread made by Darling Loggins, a rather tasty pork pie from Mrs Bancroft and a bottle of bubbly cracked open by Champagne-Charlie.

'Are you two all right?' Pelly asks me. 'Only you've had faces as long as fiddles for the last few days.'

I assure her all is well but vow to confide in her at some point. She'll be able to help me, surely she will. She is the most *sensible* woman I know.

In the evening we cram into the pub for a quiz, which our team narrowly miss winning by two-and-a-half points because Mr Grigg only arrived part way into round two. The quiz master is duly shamed for naming Salisbury as the county town of Wiltshire (it's Trowbridge) and the triumphant team not only wins the beer leg but a rib of beef in the raffle.

Chapter 6

June

4 June: The bronze nymph statue glints in the morning sun. She is back!

Next door at Mr and Mrs Champagne-Charlie's, the house martins are in and out, in and out, feeding their squealing young. Up in the field, curious young heifers and steers creep up behind dog walkers and shout: 'Moo!'

All through the night, the tractors and trailers have been hard at work, trundling through the village with heavy loads of silage. They have been harvesting like ants, bringing in the silage before the rains come. There is a faint hum on the hillside - both in noise and smell - and lights like alien spaceships landing on Bluebell Hill.

The maize begins to shoot on its long journey to becoming higher than an elephant's eye.

Oh what a beautiful morning.

And Russell's crow cock-a-doodle-doos across the valley.

5 June: The summer sunshine has us all fired up and we're off for a bike ride, the theme from *A Summer Place* wafting through my headphones.

There is Mr and Mrs Sheepwash on matching Treks and matching helmets, Mr St John on a gleaming racing bike, Mr Loggins and Darling dressed up to the nines in Lycra, Ted Moult and Jamie Lee are on a tandem and there's me on a rather rusty mountain bike. There is no sign of Mr Grigg. He went off for some obscure ingredient earlier this morning for tonight's supper and isn't back yet.

As we set off on our cycle from the square (we are known as The Square Wheelers), Mr Grigg comes round the corner and gets out of his Freeloader with a red face and is short of breath. About thirty seconds later, a white Land Rover Discovery comes round the corner and Posh Totty waves like the Queen and heads down the road.

I'm getting a little bit fed up with this.

'I'll be with you in a minute,' Mr Grigg shouts. 'You head on, I'll catch you up in a bit.'

I am tempted to say that we weren't going to wait for him anyway, *bastard*, but decide keeping quiet is the more dignified response. I push off on my bike, crashing the gears as I go.

We find ourselves climbing a tough hill, with Pelly and me straggling at the back while the others forge on ahead, led by a very determined-looking Darling Loggins.

'Is everything all right with you and Mr Grigg?' Pelly says.

'Pelly,' I say, struggling in granny gear. 'You may think he is the greatest thing since wholemeal bread you've made yourself but he is the most annoying person I have ever met.'

'Don't be silly,' she says. 'You were made for each other.'

I would shake my head if it didn't expend so much energy. I'm not sure if what's she's just said is a compliment or an insult. But it's not worth spilling my heart out. Like everyone in this village, they are all blinkered when it comes to Mr Grigg. He can do no wrong as far as everyone else is concerned.

There is a cry behind of us of 'coming through, coming through' and we are overtaken by a smug Mr Grigg who then meets us at the top of the hill with a large picnic rug already laid out on the grass.

'What kept you so long?' he says.

Bastard.

6 June: It is Bunting Day in Lush Places, a Saturday in early June when our menfolk crowd around the bottom of a ladder with copious cups of coffee while one brave soul climbs to the top and puts the flags out.

The annual village fete will soon be upon us and so will the football. Oh yes, the football.

In the Grigg household, rather like during the election, we will sit on opposite sides of the fence. Mr Grigg is passionate about the game. Me? I neither understand the offside rule nor do I care. But I do like the house and the street being decorated, which happens every year whether the football is on or not.

Six men turn out this morning to put the bunting up while my neighbour Mrs Bancroft flits in and out of her front door with a tray of coffee and biscuits. A short man stands on the phone box while a taller man balances precariously on the litter bin next to the village green in an attempt to tie a string of bunting on to a signpost. Mr Grigg is up a ladder in slippers and Mr Sheepwash swings out of an upstairs window to greet him. Part of me wants Mr Grigg to come crashing down onto the tarmac below and another part of me is completely disinterested.

The health and safety devil would have a field day if he were to cast his net right now.

The men abandon the idea of attaching bunting to the frame of the play equipment. Last year the children decided it was a great game to jump off the swings in mid-air and make a grab for individual flags of the world as they fell, with extra points for Germany. Sadly, though, Mr Grigg has not given up on his plan to attach flags to the Freeloader, which means I probably won't be driving it until the World Cup is over.

'Think yourself lucky it's not your knicker elastic he's using,' I was told last night in the pub by Hawkeye.

Roaring with laughter at his own wit when Mr Grigg expressed puzzlement, Hawkeye drawled: 'Well, if you opened the window, zoom, her'd be out.'

At that point, the conversation turned to Ferdinand and King. I thought they were talking about Spanish history.

Come on England!

9 June: In cosy cottages, council houses, mansions and farms in The Enchanted Village, there are bits of bodies everywhere.

The odd head here, a limb there. A ginger wig, lots of stuffing and chicken wire. In the Grigg household there is a headless mannequin, standing in the shadows waiting for something to happen.

Cunning plans are taking shape. And it's not my plans to quietly tear Mr Grigg apart limb from limb. No, it's the village scarecrow festival.

Over the years, we've had politics (Maggie Thatcher), football (an England football fan surrounded by lager cans), events in history (Nell Gwynne), flights of fancy (The Red Baron) and characters from children's books and TV (The BFG and Homer and Bart Simpson).

The annual event taxes brains, ingenuity, artistic ability and lateral thinking. If the best way to make a head is doing paper mache around a balloon, how do you make the neck and then secure it to the torso? And can you be bothered to make hands if you can use gloves instead? And if it sits down or leans out of a window, will that save you from making a pair of legs?

Oh, the thought that goes into it.

The standard is extremely high and every time I say 'it's the taking part that counts', the always competitive Mr Grigg rolls his eyes. If winning means that much to him, he should make the bloody thing.

Mr Loggins and Champagne-Charlie are both new kids on the block and have just popped into the Grigg house looking for ideas. The latter is doing a poacher and hopes to bag a couple of rabbits from Celebrity Farmer's fields to use as props in the scarecrow's pocket. Such attention to detail.

Bubbles says why bother doing a scarecrow at all when her husband can sit outside the house instead?

Meanwhile, in our house, the pale-looking mannequin lurks like a headless ghost. Our mannequin is disabled, courtesy of the lady vicar who, a few years ago for reasons unknown, borrowed the body and then brought it back without its right hand. Mr Grigg made a crude remark about why she would want to keep the hand. When she got married a year later, he suggested she really didn't have a need for all those extra digits and should bring the hand back. I have to say I didn't understand what he was talking about. But then I have led a very sheltered life.

12 June: The sun is shining as I take the spaniels out for their morning walk across the fields. They spring through the long grass and buttercups and plantain, flicking up the dew as they pass.

Russell's Crow yells across the valley and down on the school allotment, there is a curious structure with what looks like a stuffed body in long trousers and braces. In kitchens and front rooms, the scarecrows are finally taking shape, ready to be placed outside the house at 10 o'clock.

Mr Grigg is up at the village hall, ovens at the ready, preparing for the village Big Breakfast. He will be in charge of a kitchen full of lovelies, doing his best Gordon Ramsay impression while I sit out front and take the money. Maths is not my forte, but I'd rather be overcharging impatient customers than be anywhere near Mr Grigg in a busy kitchen.

He will bark and yell and the ladies will love him, as will the male helpers but not in a homoerotic way, you understand.

In our hallway, there is a roll-a-penny board propped up against the wall, boxes of marked-up tombola prizes and a large beer barrel. So far, preparation for the village fete today is going very smoothly. Too smoothly, methinks.

The village parade, led by the standard bearer from the Royal British Legion, is accompanied by cittern, sitar and double bass, courtesy of our record producer friend, Ding Dong Daddy. Village organisations file behind, with shields bearing the name of their groups held high.

And on the village green I can see trouble brewing as a booth selling kisses has a long line of men queued up outside it. There's Mr Loggins, Champagne-Charlie, Celebrity Farmer and Mr Sheepwash.

'Who's in the booth?' I ask Pelly. She is wearing a straw boater and is dishing up ice cream to a strange looking man with cross eyes and his left hand jiggling up and down in his pocket.

'Who do you think?' she says. 'Your friend Posh Totty. Your husband has been in there for ages.'

Bastard.

15 June: Mr Grigg and I are speaking again, but only just. He told me this morning that when he was out with the dogs he came so close to a deer they almost kissed. He seems to be making a habit of getting up close and personal to elegant creatures. He says the animal strolled boldly through the long grass, unaware its movements were being tracked. It woke from its dream with a startle and fled before Mr Grigg had the chance to say hello.

The next day, he was driving up the hill when a lumbering creature the size of a domestic cat walked in front of the car. He slowed down to see a brown hare ambling tortoise-like across the road. It stopped on the grass verge and glanced up as he passed before it turned round and disappeared into the horse daisies.

This evening, heading out for a match with the Mapperton Marauders. Mr Grigg goes up to the attic to find his cap and cricket box. He pulls it out of the bag and finds a mouse has got there first. The cricket box is nibbled neatly around the edges.

It could have been worse. The mouse might still have been in it when Mr Grigg put the thing on.

Ouch. That would have served him right.

20 June: The sound of ladders being extended against stone walls fills the square this morning as the Lush Places bunting is taken down.

It coincides with a lull in the football, a realisation that England will not win the World Cup, no matter how many times Mr Grigg wears his football shirt without washing it in between matches.

To be honest with you, I'm of the 'don't care' variety, although it would be good to have the buzz of winning in our ears instead of those damned vuvuzelas. I remember 1966 with a warm glow. Geoff Hurst was my pin-up and those pink and yellow flying saucer sweets were my favourite food.

I was only four at the time.

Yes, it would be nice for the England team to defy the odds and live to emerge from the tunnel another day, skipping hand-in-hand with their coach.

But I can't helping thinking the coalition we have now would seize upon it as yet another victory for the ConDems.

No, surely not.

Hush my mouth before Mr Grigg tapes a St George's cross over it.

Come on Inger-land!

25 June: Now that the vivid yellow of oil seed rape has disappeared from the horizon, and the lingering smell of damp bandages has fled along with it, there is a lovely sheen of blue beginning to appear in the fields.

The crop is linseed and it is beautiful. I don't see it in Lush Places, the sight greets me now on my way into work at the Death Star, along with cut hay fields and dusty roads. At home the elderflower is in full cry, the campions are going ragged around the edges and the long, long grasses sway in the breeze while the rigid, rusty docks compete with the nettles for air.

26 June: I don't really like my job much, although it's sometimes nice to get away. You can have too much of a good thing (as I keep telling Mr Grigg rather pointedly) and every now and then you need to distance yourself from it to make you realise you're not so badly off after all.

We're sleeping, on and off, in separate rooms. I don't like it much but it's good when we make up. I still can't come out with it and confront him. I'm afraid of hearing the answer. So we niggle and prod each other to the point of argument and then storm off. It's not good. I should just tell him how I feel but I can't. I'm afraid of what he might tell me. I fear he has eyes for another. He is making a fool of himself.

Chapter 7

July

7 July: My nicotianas, nasturtiums, tall spikes of yellow loosestrife, passion flowers and snapdragons and tomatoes face up to the bizzy-lizzies and red pelargoniums in the concrete pots next to the village pump on the other side of the Square.

One nil to my display, I think.

10 July: When the most exciting thing to happen in the village this week is a car going the wrong way up the one-way street, a Gold Party at the new girlfriend of Mr St John is a must. It is circled in red on the calendar.

She has asked us to take along any old bits of jewellery we no longer want. A gold expert will weigh it and then offer us a fair price. We can enjoy a glass of wine, nibbles, a natter and buy costume jewellery made by a very talented young lady from Axminster. I don't get invited to things like this very often. Never been a girlie girl, never been a lady who lunches, always too busy working. So I ransack the bedroom to find very little gold, apart from a Jersey milk bottle top, a pair of Monsoon bikini bottoms and an old bracelet from Argos.

The doorbell rings and I leave a grumbling Mr Grigg at home (how hard can it be to warm up last night's risotto?) to be accompanied by Ladies in Linen - Pelly, Darling Loggins, The Fragrant Mrs Putter, Mrs Champagne-Charlie, Mrs Bancroft and her neighbour, Night Nurse, who thinks she ought to have put her gold in a metal briefcase chained to her arm 'just for safety's sake'.

'What if someone mugs us?' she says, as we walk arm in arm along the quiet street and past the nymph, which I swear is winking. Thankfully, in Lush Places there has never been a mugging. It is not that sort of place.

Posh Totty and Jamie Lee are late and weighed down like the Brinks Mat robbers. I push my Argos bracelet deep inside my handbag, knock back two glasses of sauvignon blanc and buy a handmade necklace for £8.50.

I know my place.

14 July: A queue snakes around the village hall car park. Morris dancers with blacked-out faces wave their hankies and dance gaily around the tarmac. Inside, a sound check is carried out and the beautiful voice of a singing woman soars through the evening air.

My friend Tuppence opens the doors - a feat in itself because she's so tiny - and the crowd rushes in, making for the bar and a barrel of Branscombe Brewery's best bitter.

At the counter is Nobby Odd-Job and Mr Loggins while Pelly, Mr Sheepwash and Mrs Bancroft and I dispense the drinks in the background.

The music acts as a disembodied soundtrack to the pouring of wine and beer. It's like *The World from My Window: The Movie*. On stage is Ding Dong Daddy, tonight's promoter, with assorted members of his band The Imagined Village.

To the ringing of Mr St John's little wooden till, John Jones from Oysterband takes to the stage, after walking sixteen miles from Lyme Regis with a jolly but reluctant band of ramblers to get here. John usually has great weather for his walks to gigs. But, as usual, The Enchanted Village of Lush Places is shrouded in mist.

Through the serving hatch I can see the toes of Mamma Mia tapping, alongside Manual and Mrs Regal Bird. General Custer, who won the lottery a few years ago, asks loudly for another pint of beer, but no-one minds because Ding Dong has just described him as a legend for loaning his field for the night to happy campers.

I also get a public thank you, for helping with the PR, and I am unmasked as 'the village blogger'.

'We all have pseudonyms,' Ding Dong tells the audience. 'I'm known as Mr Charmer. If you get the chance, have a look at it. It's called The View from my Window.'

The only time I have my five minutes' of fame and someone gets my blog's name wrong.

In between the rush at the bar, we listen to the lovely singing of Jackie Oates – 'Pam Ayres with a bit of The Cranberries', according to Mr Sheepwash - as Nobby Odd-Job sits on the counter, a satisfied beam on his face for having spearheaded such a smoothly-run bar. Pelly is resting her back and sitting on a child's wooden chair in the corner of the kitchen while Mrs Bancroft is pleased with herself for mastering a special trick I taught her when pouring fizzy drinks to avoid the bubbles rising up and spilling over the top.

Mr Grigg, of course, is nowhere to be seen.

17 July: The wind is howling. Children leaving primary school for the very last time are howling.

Mrs Bancroft's hanging basket has come crashing down, along with the clematis on the wall. Posh Totty has got a fire going and it's still only six o'clock.

Ding Dong Daddy marches down the road for a swift pint, as if keeping to the beat of an integral iPod playing world music inside his polished head. The Union Flag outside the shop has wrapped itself around so many times it looks like a patriotic barber's pole.

Nobby Odd-Job drives by in his Range Rover, with its personalised number plate, and wearing a suit. The great trees on the village green bend and sway like the pictures you seen when the Caribbean has a hurricane.

Noel Edmonds plays mind games with Celebrity Farmer who sits beside his phone, waiting for the call that will tell him if he has made it on to *Deal or No Deal*. A blue plastic bag filled with dog doings lies on the edge of one of his fields.

A holidaymaking couple cross the square hand-in-hand. The brassy blonde woman looks old enough to be the man's mother.

Four boys about to go into their second year of secondary school swagger by with bicycles and footballs, looking forward to September when they can boss the younger ones around. They snigger and quietly make rude remarks about a visiting family who go past them with a pushchair.

Silky volvar toadstools have sprung up on a pile of wood chippings outside Pelly's house as the sky gets darker.

There is a sense of foreboding in the air. Here comes the summer.

20 July: It is overcast here today in Lush Places. Little pockets of sunshine occasionally break through the clouds. The trees gently rustle in memory of the great winds that blew through them over the weekend. A cow wails like a whale along the ridge above the allotments.

Despite a distinctly unpromising start, there has been plenty going on. We were invited to a chilly, chilli barbecue at the Logginses' new home. The conversation inevitably turned to logs.

A veil of boredom suddenly fell over the women's faces. A sleepy Sheepwashlet face nearly landed in the *semifreddo*.

Mrs Darling Loggins glared at her husband. 'Can we talk about something else other than bloody logs? When we go to bed at night you even read the chainsaw catalogue.'

'Well hark at you,' Mr Loggins retorted. 'It's better than reading one of your fancy books and sitting up in bed with a buttoned-up nightie like Queen Victoria.' (Mrs Loggins is well educated).

Nobby Odd-Job intervened and confided rather helpfully that his bedtime reading was the *Screwfix* catalogue. The supper then degenerated with Mr Loggins' exceptional Professor Stanley Unwin impersonations and a rendition of 'Old Mrs Hunt with a rough-cut punt'.

18 July: I've just come back from my son's graduation ceremony. It was one of the proudest moments of my life. Hundreds of Harry Potter cloaks and a great hall straight out of Hogwarts, just yards from where Number One Son studied environmental geoscience at Bristol University.

The organ played Bach and the masters in their assorted coloured cloaks and hats took to the stage dressed as Dumbledore and Co.

And I stood with my boy in his gown, had my photograph taken and smiled sweetly at his father but through gritted teeth. I wished Mr Grigg were here.

Back in the village, however, something is not quite right. My morning dog walks are usually punctuated by the sound of Russell's Crow across the valley, cocka-doodle-dooing. But not any longer.

While I was away, the noisy blighter discovered the invisibility cloak. He is no more. He is a dead bird. He has gone to meet his maker.

The end was short and sweet, I am told. And he went very well with a glass of red wine, apparently, with Bellows Packman declaring (very loudly) IT WAS THE FINEST BIRD HE HAD EVER TASTED.

But I can't help thinking the ghost of Russell's Crow might still be heard as the sun rises over The Enchanted Village. Or perhaps pecking at the windows of Bellows Packman...

21 July: The wild honesty is going to seed and the rose bay willow herb is losing its spikes of cerise flowers, like a sparkler in reverse. The clouds lie in still layers as the sun goes down, illuminating the witch on a broomstick weather vane on the house down the path.

It is the middle of July in The Enchanted Village but it feels much later. The children have almost broken up but it could be the end of August. The parched fields are damp with much-needed rain and in the mornings the mist hangs over Bluebell Hill like a shroud.

But hark, what sounds are coming from the village square? A rustle and tinkle, the clash of sticks and a jolly accordion under a colourful umbrella. The Wessex Morris Men are on tour. But there is cacophony in the wings. Never mind morris dancing waking the earth and bringing forth new life. The noise is enough to wake the dead.

They've only gone and chosen to perform on the bellringers' weekly practice night.

Hankies wave furiously as the church bells ding and dong.

A small crowd gathers. Someone goes up to the bell tower to have a quiet word. The church bells stop and the tower captain comes down to watch the Morris Men. Half an hour goes by and their performance is over.

The big bells resume. Harmony is restored.

23 July: A grey mist hangs over Lush Places. It is not unusual, but it feels chilly, like an overcoat left in a cold hallway and then put on bare arms.

A tramp is booted out of the church after a lady doing the flowers discovers him relieving himself behind the organ. The incident leaves a blemish both physically and emotionally. It is not very nice. He is no gentleman of the road.

But the greyness seems apt for the news that greets me when I come back to the village from work this afternoon. One of my blog characters has to be removed from the cast list. Poor old Dudley, he of the Grand Marnier, red wine and Guinness, he of the magic musical fingers and beautiful mind, the organiser of jazz concerts in the church and in the hall, has gone to meet his maker.

Dudley was a troubled soul who everyone knew but no-one really knew very well. He was part and parcel of everyday life in The Enchanted Village, even though he would leave us for weeks on end to get away from it all.

The last time I saw him to speak to, he was in good spirits. The two of us were deep in conversation outside the pub while he had a fag and I escaped from the World Cup. He was looking forward to a new life in the Malvern Hills - a pipe dream, maybe, who knows - but he kept expressing his gratitude for the friendship he had found in The Enchanted Village even though sometimes being here was just all too much.

I understood his need to escape – hell, every now and then I want to disappear, especially at the moment - and was pleased to see him looking so happy and making plans. He had a new spring in his step.

Sir Edward Elgar, that most English of all composers for whom the Malverns were such an inspiration, said: 'My idea is that there is music in the air, music all around us, the world is full of it and you simply take as much as you require.'

Rest in peace Dudley, The Enchanted Village will miss you.

Chapter 8

August

3 August: Even on the wastelands there is beauty to be found. The bindweed weaves its way up through a chain link fence, its tightly clasped flowers ready to unfurl into great white trumpets. Up above, a nodding bramble bears blackberries of green, red and black.

Down on Mr Grigg's plot, there is fruit to be had. Blackcurrants in abundance, their smell on being picked taking me back to the 1970s when I earned thirty five pence a bucket during the summer holidays. Crushed purple blackness on dextrous fingers.

The gooseberry bush with fruits we have missed – skeletal branches with fat and spiky globes hanging like pendants – and the odd raspberry, just one each, as a mouthwatering precursor to the harvest ahead.

August, the month of the long school holidays, daily plant watering, haymaking and my birthday. Perfect.

7 August: As I sit here, the most beautiful piano music is coming from the stereo. I wish you could hear it: it's got a gentle, rising melody, sad chords and builds up to a hopeful and happy ending. It sounds like a film score. It was composed and played by Dudley, who was buried yesterday in the village churchyard.

As the many mourners filed out behind his coffin, I picked up one of his CDs his family requested people to take.

They were astounded at the turn-out of villagers.

'We didn't realise he knew so many people,' his cousin said.

It was a typical Enchanted Village day, with that misty mizzle swirling through the rooftops and in and out of the church gates.

'He had his problems but we all loved him,' I said. 'He was Dudley. We'll miss him.'

The church was full of the great and the good, villagers, eccentrics and even a tramp, who had scrubbed up well for the day. He looked bewildered as he gazed out across the pews but here he was an equal. Behind me, an elderly gentleman with a big bushy beard pulled out a tie and belt from a small white suitcase and proceeded to change and comb his hair.

Night Nurse, behind him, was fascinated.

'Look at his hand. Those long fingers. Beautiful hands,' she said.

I looked around and everyone was there: Mamma Mia, Celebrity Farmer, Mr F Word and Camilla, Posh Totty and MDF Man, Hawkeye, Dudley's dear pal Caruso, Super Mario, Pelly and Mr Sheepwash, Mrs Bancroft, the Putters, Nobby Odd-Job, Bellows, Ding Dong Daddy, Tuppence and two sets of ex-publicans.

In the pub afterwards, Mr Grigg drank so much he fell over and crashed into a table. A combine harvester went the wrong way up the one-way street outside the window. The village shop where Dudley used to go in early and do the papers because he couldn't sleep, was closed while our shopkeepers attended the funeral.

Hawkeye proposed to his long-time girlfriend and the ornamental hunting horns were taken off the ceiling with the landlady leading the bugle call as she galloped around the bar.

In the corner where Dudley once sat, the high-backed chair remained empty.

Caruso sang a song and we each raised a very large glass of Grand Marnier to Dudley's memory.

Here's to you Dudley. God bless.

8 August: Mr Loggins was regaling us with a story of how a large piece of driftwood floated *Jaws*-style towards him as he sat on Burton Bradstock beach with friends.

'It was like destiny. It was coming straight for me,' he said, his mouth full of Eton Mess.

'I nearly came back home and got my chainsaw.'

11 August: Today as I walk the dogs, there is a real what I call 'a Melplash Show morning' feel to the air.

Our local agricultural show is always at the end of August and it coincides with the slight chill and morning dew that signals the onset of autumn. The hedges are damp and smell of vegetation, decaying yet fruiting all at the same time. There are muddy puddles that sparkle with a splash of anticipation as the sun comes up. A hot air balloon drifts slowly, noiselessly, effortlessly across the Enchanted Village.

It is a Ray Bradbury story, but not *Something Wicked This Way Comes*. It's called *Something Very Good Is About To Happen*.

I love the summer but I don't mourn its passing. I embrace the autumn, the change in the seasons, the constant life cycle that reminds us it's good to be alive. We are here only fleetingly but we are stardust. We are golden.

Tonight and tomorrow I will be trying to persuade Mr Grigg to come with me for an evening of adventure that will start just after midnight. I want to go to Dorset's highest point and lay the blanket on the ground and look to the skies. I want us to get back to being a couple, marvelling at the wonders of nature all around us. It will be romantic.

For this week, the Perseids, that most heavenly of meteor showers, are upon us. Astronomers say it could be the best show in years. Up to eighty meteors an hour whizzing through the night sky.

Bring it on.

12 August: So there we were, lying on our backs on the slopes of Bluebell Hill in the middle of the night. And not just the two of us. We seemed to have picked up a party of followers along the way.

'Oooh,' squealed Mrs Bancroft, as a meteor shot through the sky like a flare.

But the Perseids meteor shower, which I had so hyped to my neighbours that they ended up joining us, was a bit of a damp squib. Astronomers said it would be the best show in ages. But as eighty meteors an hour is just over one a minute, there were long periods where we just stared so hard the constellations began to dance with each other.

The most stunning sight was Jupiter, low in the south eastern sky, and shining so brightly it almost hurt our eyes.

Plastic glass of Cava in one hand, iPod in the other, I hunted around in the dark for *The Planet Suite* to mask the sound of grumbling neighbours around me in the grass.

'Fancy bringing us all the way up here just for this,' I heard Bubbles say, before I dived for cover under the blanket of Gustav Holst.

As I peered down to select the most fitting track, a shout rang out: 'Wow, that was fantastic.'

I looked up. And there was nothing. Every time I went back to the iPod to find something by The Cinematic Orchestra or Air to give me a soundtrack to a starshow, there were similar shrieks of delight on the grass around me.

So I gave up searching for the music when I inadvertently pressed Bill Haley and the Comets and had *Rock Around the Clock* blaring in both ears. I stayed absolutely still for several million light years. I saw two shooting stars. It was about as exciting as watching a distant celestial needle darning with silver thread.

Behind me, some bewildered sheep started up a baa chorus and then the flashing lights of several aeroplanes passed through the skies in quick succession.

It was the most exciting thing to happen all evening.

Weather permitting, the Perseids can be seen again tonight. And apparently, you can see Jupiter's four moons just with the aid of some decent binoculars.

Me? I think I'll be having an early night.

13 August: A dry spell in August means haymaking. The cut fields smell of my childhood, and the tractors thunder through the Square to pick up the bales before the rains come.

This week, Mr Grigg has been victorious, picking up a medal in the battle for the Crosby Plate, a major cricket competition around these parts.

The team should get a mention on Radio Four on August 25 - my birthday - when human rights lawyer Clive Stafford Smith presents *With Great Pleasure.* This is a *Desert Island Discs*-style programme with guest presenters and literature at its heart.

I know this because on Monday, the ever-resourceful Pelly managed to get us tickets for two recordings of the show at The Electric Palace in Bridport. This is an old cinema that has risen phoenix-like from the dust of years of closure to become one of the best and most diverse entertainment venues around. Mr Grigg cried off to play cricket. Or so he said.

I feared an intense, highbrow performance from Stafford Smith, who for 25 years has been representing prisoners facing the death penalty. He is a very clever man. But he strolled on to the stage in cricket whites, and with self-deprecating humour apologised for his appearance. He explained he was hoping to catch the last minutes of a cricket final in a nearby village. He was playing for the Mapperton Marauders.

I gave a big whoop. This is Mr Grigg's team and he was its founding captain ten years ago and is still playing for them. Listen in at 11.30am when the show is broadcast. You may just hear me whooping.

Stafford Smith's choice of prose and poetry was highly accessible. It made perfect sense when he confided that, as a child, the mythical character with whom he most identified was Robin Hood. A fearless campaigner for social justice, he is the founder and director of Reprieve, which uses the law to enforce the human rights of prisoners from death row to Guantánamo Bay. One of the most poignant pieces he chose was a statement by a right wing US judge who at the eleventh hour of his professional life suddenly wandered down a humanitarian path.

Then it was the turn of Fay Weldon, who toddled on to the stage in black top and velvet trousers and a magnificent technicolour dreamcoat jacket. Despite her advancing years and constant putting on and removing large glasses at the microphone, she was as sharp as Mr Grigg's penknife. In a sweet, posh voice, she told the audience this was a Radio Four first as her interview with Roy Plumley for *Desert Island Discs* was never broadcast. Hers was indeed a more highbrow choice, with a Thomas Hardy poem thrown in for the Dorset audience.

At the end of the show, we ambled up to the town hall where an army of Mapperton Marauders were outside a pub, celebrating their win with cider and roll-ups. Back home, Mr Grigg would be in good spirits and the diet forgotten, so Mrs Bancroft, Number One Son and I went to the chip shop to pick up some supper.

As we waited for our haddock to cook, who should stroll in for a piece of fish but Fay Weldon, her naughty eyes a-glinting. The old she-devil.

14 August: Thinking of Fay Weldon's abortive *Desert Island Discs* programme, I have always been a great one for compiling lists of favourite records. If I ever became famous, what records would I choose? My tastes are eclectic, but I've always come up with the same ones: *Jupiter* from The Planet Suite, Norman Greenbaum's *Spirit in the Sky*, George McCrae and *Rock Ya Baby* and these days probably *To Build a Home* by the Cinematic Orchestra and Faure's *Sicilienne*. I might throw in a Somerset folk song to acknowledge my heritage and then probably a bit of new wave to show my age.

But after last night, I've been thinking about books, and the books or pieces of writing that have been with me for some years.

I put the romantic side of my nature down to the books I was reading or had read to me when I was a child. At the age of about six, my older sister read me *Don Quixote* – 'Quicks-oat', she said – which I didn't really understand but it put pictures in my mind. *Tales of Long Ago* by Enid Blyton filled me with stories of the Greek myths. I was very fond of *The Princess and the Goblin*, *The Secret Garden* and especially the Narnia chronicles.

I was also very partial to fairytales by the Brothers Grimm.

It explains a lot, I think.

17 August: You can tell things are a bit better between us when I rant about different things other than my infuriating husband, who has not been disappearing so much lately. There are only a few things I dislike. And offal, bureaucracy, bad manners and the destruction of natural beauty and the built environment are some of them.

I am a girl in love with her surroundings. It wounds me deeply when things are changed and not for the better.

Well three of my pet hates have just happened here in Lush Places, right under our noses. One day, while no-one was looking, two council workmen turned up and installed six bollards in front of the listed building next door. It now looks like a mini-version of Avebury. But unlike the mysterious stone circles of that famous Wiltshire village, this one is a semi-circle of the black plastic variety.

This is a village square with historical features that include an old pub, a commemorative plaque, a village pump and a red telephone box. It is quintessentially English.

Bubbles, who is so lovingly restoring the Champagne-Charlie house, wailed: 'I can't believe they can just do that without telling anyone. If they had to do it, you'd think they would put in something more in keeping.'

I feel like force-feeding the bureaucrats with offal.

21 August: A blanket of mizzle smothers The Enchanted Village. Pairs of grumpy jackdaw babies, feathers ruffled, huddle on chimney pots. Swallows, trying desperately to be cheerful, swoop low to the ground in search of food. They dart in and out of the damp cattle, attempting to stir up some frivolity in the misty rain and peasouper fog.

Along the road in the next village, the weather has washed out fun day. Down in Bridport, carnival organisers are looking to the skies in advance of tonight's procession. Their hands are outstretched as they ask themselves 'why us?'

Over the hill, *Doc Martin* and *Men Behaving Badly* star Martin Clunes is anxious for tomorrow. For the past year, he and his family have been planning their horse and dog show at Buckham Down. It raises thousands for the local hospice and comes complete with funfair and squid tent run by the Riverside Restaurant at West Bay.

Clunes has secured the most wonderful publicity for his fair, both locally and nationally, with page leads in the local papers and a front page feature in today's Daily Telegraph Weekend section. He's even got AA yellow signs pointing to his event.

But even he can't control the weather. The British summer.

Don't you just love it?

25 August: It's my birthday today and it's raining. It never rains on my birthday.

There's a time and a place for everything.

The seagulls are swirling inland, caw, caw, cawing, far away from stormy waters. The rooks dive-bomb a hovering buzzard and a passing car crunches an ambling snail.

And downstairs, Mr Grigg is exercising to his hero, Bob Dylan, and *Thunder on the Mountain*.

My mother recalls the moment forty nine years ago when she went out to the cowstalls at six-thirty, to take my father his morning cup of tea. A short while later, she bedded down in our front room and gave birth to me, the youngest of five (and only one of them a boy) at a quarter to nine.

When my father came in for breakfast the midwife told him he'd had another daughter. Family folklore says he turned round and headed back to the cowstalls. But I was the youngest and spoilt rotten. Brown eyes like coal and nicknamed 'Sausage' because I was so deliciously fat. I was a terrific sulker who would dive under the nearest table if I didn't get my own way. I once poured milk into the Roberts wireless because no-one was listening to me.

It still happens now occasionally – the table trick, I mean. I'm tempted to do it this morning in protest at the rain.

After opening my cards (with an especially slushy one from Mr Grigg who gives me the biggest kiss in years) I drive to work along the top road next to the BBC World Service masts. But I give the radio a miss, listening instead to my birthday CDs, The Incredible Bongo Band and funk and soul classics from the 80s, the water spraying in my wake as I bellow to Chaka Khan.

It can rain all it likes. Today is a good day.

28 August: As we sit around the village hall, wearing sparkly outfits, pens and bingo cards on tables, Mr Grigg walks in with a pair of black, glittery wings strapped to his back. Tonight, Matthew, he becomes bingo caller for the evening, operating a very noisy toy machine made from plastic.

It's a fundraising event organised by our fete committee, of which Mr Grigg and I are a part.

'On its own...sixteen' he calls from the stage, much to everyone's confusion.

'Two fat ladies...seventy six.'

'What?' yells Mamma Mia from the back.

'Top of the shop...soixante neuf,' Mr Grigg shouts, with a schoolboy grin.

The vice-chairman of the parish council nearly falls off his chair.

'House!' Manual shrieks, and is promptly presented with the top prize of a lettuce.

It gets better. One table wins ice lollies for a line and Mrs Bancroft is told off for cheating in musical chairs after doing a scissor jump to an empty seat on the other side. The crowd walks casually along the line of chairs to The Who's *My Generation*. Monty Chocs-Away, with moustache waxed just for the evening, walks backwards and trips over Night Nurse.

Bellows gives a very sincere vote of thanks to the group, saying ours is the most important in the village.

'YOU'RE THE LIFEBLOOD,' he shouts. 'YOU BRING EVERYONE TOGETHER.'

I almost cry.

At the end of the evening, we clear up and Bing Crosby's dulcet tones come across on my amplified iPod, singing *Don't Fence Me In*. The Andrews Sisters are joined on harmonies by me, Mrs Bancroft, Night Nurse and Pelly Sheepwash, who earlier I had made sure won musical chairs because I was doing the music.

And then *Jailhouse Rock* comes on and Mrs Bancroft starts playing air guitar and I dance around the room, jiving with a chair.

What we don't appreciate is that Mrs Bancroft's son-in-law is filming the entire thing on his phone and will put it on YouTube tomorrow.

29 August: As I prepare my photographic entries for tomorrow's village show, I can see from inside that outside there is a rain soaked sky beginning to turn blue. The phone rings. It's Mr Sheepwash.

'Go outside,' he says. 'There's a rainbow.'

'And..?'

'It's *upside down*.'

Sure enough, there is a prismatic smile overhead. Even the gods are smiling. I could be on to a winner for tomorrow's show.

30 August: It is the day of the flower show. Car boots are open on the hall forecourt, spilling out dahlias, leeks the length of Chile and spikes of gladioli sharp enough to impale yourself on. Gardeners, bakers, photographers and handicraft makers walk into the hall steadily, carefully, so as not to trip.

A gardener from Lush Corners, The Enchanted Village's smaller neighbour, clutches a mother-in-law's tongue and peeks out from the stiff leaves to find her way in through the lobby, which is lined with decorated paper plates all in a class of their own.

She is annoyed with herself because she has left her tomatoes and her longest runner bean at home and time is running out.

There is muttering over marrows too heavily polished and slurpy-looking jam. A late entry is brought in by a tousled-looking woman who stayed up until three-thirty this morning playing Pictionary, making buttonholes and cooking chutney.

Over on the photographic table, people surreptitiously swap their entries around, hoping their top left spot will make their picture stand out that much more than the opposition. People new to the village are eyed suspiciously, as they bring in beautifully decorated cakes and artwork good enough to line the walls of Sladers Yard at West Bay. Bloody incomers.

This year I have submitted eight pictures in the photographic section. I am hoping for success with my entry in the 'wildlife' category. It's a close-up of one of the pub regulars, General Custer, pointing at the camera. He has a face carved from Mount Rushmore and hair of steel grey wire.

It could win, I tell him, agreeing to split the prize money if it does.

His eyes light up.

'That'll be all of 20p then,' I say.

Winning entry? I should be so lucky.

Chapter 9

September

1 September: As the swallows preen themselves, making last minute preparations for their flight south, the water gurgles and burbles down the street. A burst main, ignored by the water board.

Across the road, the new water feature behind the gated gravelled drive of Monty Chocs-Away echoes in frustration on its endless, tinkling cycle. It yearns to be free like the youthful tributary in the road.

Super Mario is up a ladder, attending to the latest set of village window frames that could do with a lick of paint. Posh Totty gives me a cheery wave as she heads off in the white Land Rover to feed her horses.

I walk through the hayfield and pick up some of the last hay of the season, freshly turned. I put it to my nose, breathe in deeply and smell the last days of summer and the early days of my childhood.

In the next field, the maize is as tall as a dinosaur and the path through it is unfamiliar, sinister, until you see the light at the end of the tunnel, the gateway down from Bluebell Hill and beyond. Arrows point both ways on the handmade signboard. Every which way but loose.

It is a like a scene from Hitchcock's *North by Northwest.* Any minute, I expect a crop dusting plane to appear from nowhere as Cary Grant and Eva Marie Saint burst through the maize across my path.

'Oh, it's Roger Thornhill,' I will say and Cary will sweep me off my feet and kiss me, and Eva will look put out, because I am the first person in the whole film not to have mistaken him for CIA agent George Kaplan.

I emerge from the maize disappointed, only to find some nonchalant sheep grazing in the evening sun.

I pass a young man with a ring through his eyebrow accompanied by two giddy schoolgirls on their way up to the maize field.

'Awryte?' he says. He is no Cary Grant.

I make my way back up the road. A giant wooden toadstool put out for the rubbish men by Ted Moult and Jamie Lee gathers fungus outside their front gate.

And still the water burbles and gurgles down the street.

3 September: Tractors towing trailers full of potatoes have been thundering through the village over the past few days. We initially thought it was Mrs Bancroft's supply for a mass baked potato supper but it transpires they are on their way to become Walkers crisps. Mr Grigg and I have been lying in wait for them next to the speed bumps, our arms outstretched, in the hope of catching a few strays.

I remember seeing a potato trailer going up a hill once, the tractor driver oblivious as the spuds escaped and rolled out cheerfully in his wake. Like something from medieval times, locals came out of their front doors to scoop up their rewards. That happened with a meat lorry in Chard years ago when I was on a school lunch break. It did a U-turn, its back doors flew open and joints fired out in all directions. I have never seen so many 1970s teenagers act so quickly, running out into the street en masse, picking up legs of lamb, chickens and rib of beef and scuttling home to mother with enough food to feed the family for a week.

9 September: It is morning in The Enchanted Village. The church clock strikes eight and then a reversing bus goes 'peep...peep...peep' as it does a three-point turn in the square. This has been its manoeuvre ever since a gung-ho driver thought he could get round the corner of the one-way system and shaved several stones off the pub wall in the process.

A small blind terrier yap-yap-yaps at nothing in particular as he scuttles along to the village shop with his elderly (also blind) owner.

Secondary school age children swagger down to the bus, great big backpacks swinging from their shoulders. A short while later the smaller ones, holding their mothers' hands, walk down to the village school. I see Pelly Sheepwash dawdling as if she were being dragged to work by some invisible force. Bellows barges past the house, 'LATE FOR WORK AS USUAL'.

The pelargoniums in front of the village pump are losing their vigour. They look as if they are a withering bunch of flowers placed there for a crash victim.

It is autumn in Lush Places, where the seasonal cycle dictates that everything must change but, on the grand scale of things, nothing actually does. The fields are beginning to fill up with crunchy leaves, churned-up mud and magic mushrooms. The blackberries slowly ripen and the blackthorn branches are heavy with sloes. The spaniels chase the rabbits zig-zagging through the grass. The log piles are stacked up and the heating engineers' vans arrive to service the village Agas and Rayburns.

The mobile library, with its knowledgeable and kindly librarian, will be pulling up outside the house soon. And Mr Grigg, who has taken the week off to finish the decorating, has just fired up Bob Dylan's *Thunder on the Mountain*, ready for his daily workout.

Some things never change.

5 September: As you know, from my window, you can see the village square. It isn't typically English in the traditional sense - there is no market cross in the middle. But, you will remember, we have a village pump that people gossip around, a shop, a pub, a red telephone box and a village green behind a picket fence.

The square is bounded by old cottages, mostly dating back to Victorian times but, in the case of the Grigg hovel, the crick frame inside indicates its sixteenth century origins. There is a plaque on a cottage wall commemorating the visit in 1651 of a king on the run from the Roundheads.

It is an interesting square, a focal point, and many of the buildings are listed. You have to jump through various hoops in triplicate before you are allowed to carry out alterations. And quite right too.

However, if you are the county council, you can do what you like. In recent years we have had modern street lights that look like the monsters from the *War of the Worlds* movie. The lamp posts muster in the square and then march down the road.

Some weeks ago, black plastic bollards appeared from nowhere and were put on the pavement in front of a handsome stone house - ostensibly to stop people from parking on it, although a quiet word would have done the trick.

And now? Oh, you would not believe it. A white crescent of sand has materialised in front of the shop. It is meant to delineate where cars can park. But the talk in the pub is that the village has been taken over by the bureaucrats.

There is also a crescent of the same white sand in front of the house next door where cars can't park and then a long sandbar down to the school in lieu of a pavement.

Villagers want to set up a beach volleyball team to play on the sand under the floodlights. They want to get a photo of themselves in deckchairs, sunglasses and knotted handkerchiefs and send it to the *Daily Mail*.

The way this saga has unfolded in the Enchanted Village is a prime example of how not do it.

'How dare they spoil our village,' said one local.

'They don't have to *live* here,' wailed another.

And I'm feeling a little bit guilty because I hate the bureaucrats for doing this yet I'm happy enough to accept a pay cheque from them at the end of each month.

Meanwhile, up the road on the village outskirts, where Bellows and his community-minded team have restored an unloved football field, the story is the other way round. The children, quite naturally, use a shortcut to get to the field. So Bellows and crew have carved out steps so they can still come and go. His team of parents has put up a wooden fence 'crash' barrier to stop the youngsters running out in the road and being flattened by speeding cars.

The same council has come down on them like a ton of sand. The fence is too close to the highway, apparently.

The reaction here?

Bollards.

7 September: This evening, I tear in from work, take the dogs for a tour around the maize field, stop off to give Pelly Sheepwash a cashmere scarf of turquoise blue, then ring the fragrant Mrs Putter about a book club she and I are going to run this autumn.

Both book lovers, but nothing too heavy (*War and Peace* brought me the onset of early labour resulting in Number One Son 21 years ago), we've decided to experiment with the circle of six. The rest of the club consists of dear Mrs Bancroft (I love her), Pelly (of course), Darling Loggins (who scares me, just a little bit) and Mrs Champagne-Charlie (who, I hope, will be in charge of liquid refreshments).

So Book Club begins next month but not before Mrs Putter and I get together to discuss ground rules later this week. It is our idea, after all, so what we say goes.

Anyway tonight, Mr Grigg comes home from work, accompanied by Mr Loggins whom he has found loitering outside. I have no time for chit chat, there is a pan of brown rice boiling on the stove and a washing machine full of whites ready to go. So I strip Mr G of his work shirt while he is in deep conversation and then, when the doorbell rings, dare him to answer it half naked because I know it will be Mrs Bancroft to collect me for our new singing group, my latest Big Idea.

This is the new choir set up after a drunken conversation between Caruso and me in the pub at Dudley's wake a few weeks ago. We are going to the old people's community hall to learn folk songs. What my fellow songsters do not realise is that there is to be a public performance at Christmas in our village hall, at an event featuring Mr Loggins and his merry band of Mummers and Mr Folk-Record-Producer, aka Ding Dong Daddy.

Mr Grigg goes to the door shirtless and then heads upstairs with what sounds like Champagne-Charlie. I waltz off through the front door with baritone Mr Loggins and then turn tail when I realise I have forgotten to take the washed towels upstairs. I get upstairs to find Mr Grigg, belly-a-all-hanging-out, discussing the new flooring with the carpet fitter.

Embarrassed, I mumble something about taking the shirt off Mr Grigg's back so as not to waste the washing machine water and then head off into the darkness with another man. It all sounds a bit odd. The carpet fitter, understandably, looks a little confused and keeps a respectable distance from the Shirtless Man. He's heard all about village people.

Up at the community hall, Caruso leads a group of fifteen (not bad, for a drunken suggestion) in a collection of English folk songs.

It starts well, with *Dashing Away with the Smoothing Iron*, an apparently Somerset folk song I know from school, and then deteriorates into a litany of ditties mostly about nagging wives beaten into submission by their so-called better halves threatening them with a damn good yoking.

The faces around the semi-circle start to frown: Night Nurse scowls, Mrs Bancroft mouths the upper class equivalent of 'WTF?', Mamma Mia is thinking Abba songs would be much more fun, and my singing partner Mrs Regal Bird drops the song sheet in a coughing fit. At the end of the last verse where I am meekly meant to be singing 'cooks' I say 'cocks' by mistake.

At half time, we gorge on Caruso's home-made melting moments and Mr Putter starts singing *Donald Where's Your Troosers?* Then it's all off down the pub for a quick drink.

'Your usual?' the landlord asks me.

So after one glass of my own special wine, because I won't drink anything else, I realise Mr Grigg has the house keys. And he's up at Nobby Odd-Job's, watching England playing Switzerland.

Just as I ring Nobby's doorbell, I can hear Mr Grigg yelling as Switzerland score. I have jinxed the game. So I head off into Nobby's kitchen for a glass of wine and an opportunity to pore over the forbidden fruit of the *Daily Mail*.

11 September: On the afternoon walk, there are shiny conkers on the ground, disinterested sheep in the field and shots being fired across the valley.

The dogs limbo under the gate to greet three walkers by growling and barking at them. This is unusual, because they are usually quite polite. Then I recognise the rabbit-in-the-headlights look of one of the trio and realise the last time we met he was canvassing for my vote in the General Election.

It is Oliver Letwin, closely followed by a tall friend down for the weekend, who is trying desperately to get his phone to work.

'Fat chance, mate,' I say in my head, the words of Nigel Molesworth jumping into my ears. 'Lush Places is a signal-free zone, as any fule kno.'

I then realise the very tall man is no fule, he is Charles Moore, one-time editor of The Sunday Torygraph, The Daily Torygraph and The Spectator.

I smile because I am more civil than my dogs, which jump in the stream and then come out shaking water all over them.

Just up the lane, I see through Pelly Sheepwash's window that she's doing something on the computer. It transpires that as a union member, she is online casting her vote for the next Labour leader to replace Gordon Brown.

'I've just voted for Ed,' she says and I say: 'That's nothing, I've just seen a brace of distinguished Conservatives up your lane and there's someone up there with a shotgun and do you think before they get shot we ought to buttonhole them about the burst water main that's been spilling down the road for the last fortnight and have a whinge about the new bollards and streetlights and, while they're at it, they could have an ice cream on the new village beach?'

'Uh, no,' she says. And then a look of mischief passes across her face as she spots the Letwin-Moore wagon in her parking space outside her house.

'I'm going to get my *workers' rights* poster and stick it on their windscreen.'

19 September: As I gaze from my window across the square this morning, the white-sand 'beach' installed outside the village shop is blemished.

Splatters of scraped-up cow dung stand out like a pimple on a clear-skinned five-year-old. Mixed in with tyre prints and oil from leaking radiators, the beach installed by the council to denote where cars can park could already do with a tidy up. Luckily, today is the day of the Great Dorset Beach Clean.

Unluckily, Lush Places is just a bit too far inland. Eight miles too far.

This week the council came to paint a 'No Entry' sign on the junction outside the pub. Not to stop the boozers going in but to prevent vehicles driving the wrong way up the one-way street. The traffic lights secured for the occasion had been found in the props department of an Ealing comedy. When they were green, the cars came through from the other direction and when they were red you were expected to proceed with caution.

As one female driver waited patiently at the red light, the council workman waved his hands and shooed her on.

'What is it with these people?' he yelled to no-one in particular. 'Can't they see that red means green? Bloody women drivers.'

22 September: It's fungus foraging time in this part of Dorset, with crocodiles of woodland treasure hunters trudging up to Bluebell Hill armed with baskets, a reliable guidebook and a heart full of hope.

They are searching for the penny bun, the name we give to the Cep, that most prized of mushrooms, which lurks on the forest floor beneath ancient beech trees.

As country children growing up, my four siblings and I stuck mostly to field mushrooms on the farm, cursing the townies for getting to them before we did.

These days, the Sunday and Saturday supplements are bursting with tales of forages and forays, as if everyone's doing it. Last year, I was lucky enough to go with a friend on a fungus foray with Hugh Fearnley-Whittingstall's expert John Wright, who knows a thing or two about mushrooms. He wrote the excellent *Mushrooms: River Cottage Handbook No 1*.

John is as delighted with a close-up inspection of a tiny orange toadstool sprouting from a cow pat as he is slicing off a piece of beefsteak fungus from a tree trunk and then taking it home for tea.

He knows what he is looking for. He knows what is edible and he knows what fungi is best avoided.

If in doubt, let it lie.

The same thought came to my mind on Sunday as Mr Grigg lay sprawled out on the sofa, going greener and greener. Let him lie, I said to myself, because there was no way I was going to move him without kicking up a stink. Earlier that day, he had tizzled himself up a nice breakfast of chorizo and slivers of giant puffball, an edible and unmistakable fungus.

'Would you like some?' he asked, wafting the pan under my nose.

The greatest of all my senses is smell, closely followed by taste (which, of course, is exquisite). I can smell milk that has gone off even before it makes the life-changing decision for itself. I knew I was going to give the Puffball Surprise the cold shoulder after catching a whiff of it from sixty paces. Just the smell of it made me feel sick.

Which is exactly what Mr Grigg felt as we were heading up the motorway for a ninetieth birthday party in Bristol several hours later.

'I've got to pull over,' he said, leaping out of the car on the hard shoulder before he had even put the handbrake on.

Sick as a dog, his skin went alternate shades of green and yellow, he was hot and cold and his pulse was racing. We spent the next hour-and-a-half in the hospital accident and emergency department, in between the waiting room and the lavatory. I could picture him in there blowing up like a puffer fish or Violet Beauregarde from *Charlie and the Chocolate Factory* while the campfire song *Green and yeller* rushed around on speed inside my head.

As it was, he made a full recovery. But I am just so pleased he didn't have his puffball breakfast a day earlier. On the Saturday we had celebrated Mr Loggins' special birthday up a creek on the River Dart in a 12-man canoe.

Still, at least he wouldn't have been without a paddle.

24 September: As I write, it's a mad scramble to get things done before heading off on the annual weekend trip to North Devon.

In years gone by, there would have been a charabanc pulling up outside my house, filled with cloche-hatted ladies and men with moustaches and a kite-tail trail of freshly-scrubbed children flying (securely attached) in its wake.

But today we'll be heading for the seaside under our own steam, with some taking their time while others - like me - will be rushing.

It's the first time I've been to this weekend event, organised by Manuel and Mrs Regal Bird, and I'm not really sure what to expect. We've been told to pack our swimming costumes (striped, knitted bathing suits) and hiking boots (hobnails) and be prepared for fun and organised games.

Ooer.

I'm not much of a participant, more of a watcher or an organiser, so this could be very interesting.

In the meantime, I will leave you with the following titbits that have come to me via the Enchanted Village's jungle drums. Each of them could have made a blog post of their own. But time is tight, so you will have to weave your own descriptions around them:

1) The Over Sixties trip to Bath when a head count at pick-up time revealed one of the elderly passengers was missing. After half an hour of high drama, involving the bus going round and round the city centre because it had used up its allocated parking time and then intense scrutiny of Bath's CCTV footage by the police, the errant day tripper was traced and all was well. There is now talk of providing the entire membership with high-visibility jackets and return luggage labels.

2) There is an inquiry going on over a lemon meringue pie entered for the village flower and produce show. Simply the best, it was disqualified because the judge insisted it was too small although the rules stated it had to be 'up to' a certain size, so, in theory, it could have been as small as a biscuit. Only it wasn't, obviously. There is now talk of a lemon meringue pie fight to thrash it out next year.

3) And finally, courtesy of my good mate, Tuppence, here is a genuine advert from our local paper about a property for sale in The Enchanted Village:

Lush Places: A very attractive newly built semi-detached house in this popular Conversation village.

26 September: Sea views, paper thin walls. A band of happy, suited and booted Baptists on a weekend away wander through the hotel. Fifty-year-old Mods zoom past on a scooter rally to Woollacombe. Fred Perry shirts, Doc Martens under half-mast Levi's. Long, wistful looks at Lambrettas and Vespas. Those were the days.

Mr Loggins and Darling, body-boarding in wetsuits in between the flags on the acres-long shore of white sand. Pelly Sheepwash going into raptures at a springer spaniel puppy running and laughing along the beach, all the time looking back to make sure mum and dad are still watching.

This is The Enchanted Village annual outing. Some thirty two of us are on tour, Lush Places gone large. Out to settle old scores with a team from Trowbridge, Wiltshire.

Canteen catering, plenty for seconds. And thirds. Plates piled high.

Chips on the seafront, £4.50 for parking. Mr Grigg buys me new shoes because he's left my hiking boots at home. Or so we think.

A walk up the hill, Manual and Mrs Regal Bird stopping to give us a lift. Farmer Mayfield giggling along corridors, Mamma Mia putting my name down for every team game under the sun.

And in the afternoon, as Dorset play Wiltshire, Maddie Grigg goes up to the table skittles table and calmly takes the ball on a chain. She gently pushes it. She shoots. She scores. A heroine. All nine down at once.

Mr Grigg walks in slow motion across the bar.

'You're a star!' he shouts, as he engulfs me in a big bear hug. 'You got a flopper!'

He is in love with me all over again, just because I've got a flopper. It's something I have heard talked about for over forty years, in the skittle alleys and around the table skittles tables all over the pubs of West Dorset and South Somerset and beyond. But until this moment, I never really knew what a flopper was.

I am on cloud nine, an imagined laurel crown around my head, borne on a chariot of invisible village menfolk, toasting my legendary performance.

And then we lose to Wiltshire 14-12.

This morning, there is a quiet knock on our hotel room door and the sound of someone running away. I find a plastic bag on the floor, with my hiking boots inside. They've been in the Sheepwash's room all weekend.

Oh, the games people play.

Chapter 10

October

5 October: There is great excitement in the village square today as the bus breaks down, just at the point where the driver is doing a three-point turn. The result is even more chaos than usual, as motorists work out which way to negotiate this temporary roundabout. Initially I thought there was a fight going on because I glimpsed an angry young man with a mohican haircut and a grumpy old lady on a zimmer frame loitering around the bus door. Then I realised they were disgruntled passengers wondering how they were going to reach their destinations.

There must be more to life than this.

7 October: I have just heard there is now a pole inside the pub, brought in especially for Sunday regulars. I have visions of all the drinkers from Compost Corner gyrating around the pole while Larry the landlord gives it some welly on the karaoke machine.

It could be that the brewery is converting the pub into a fire station and the pole represents a quick exit from the rooms upstairs.

9 October: Mrs Bancroft has had her potted bay tree - the one the size of Africa - taken away from the front of her cottage and put in the garden of Nobby Odd-Job's yet-to-be-built new house. I am pleased about this because I dreamed the other night that the tree's roots had reached out, triffid-like, across the square and strangled Mr Grigg and me in our sleep. I then woke up and discovered it was the Medea Necklace.

Anyway, the bay tree was transported to Nobby's by Celebrity Farmer with a tractor and link-box. He proudly knocked on Nobby's door to say it had arrived, only for Nobby to rather ungratefully declare it was a yucca.

12 October: I have had a rather spooky experience this morning. As I walked from outside into my hallway to the living room, the eyes in the back of my head saw a hand at knee level come in around the front door and place an envelope on my window seat. I turned on my heels, flung the door open, only to find the cheerful neighbourhood watch man, the kindly colonel with a handlebar moustache and a disability scooter, making a quick getaway across the square. On inspection, the envelope contained handy hints on how to deter thieves. Number one was 'lock the door behind you' and 'beware of elderly disabled men bearing crime prevention advice'.

19 October: Something's afoot. Across the Square, the publicans Larry and Mimi hand in their notice and then our shopkeepers reveal they, too, are planning to shut the till drawer permanently just as soon as they get a buyer.

Is it something I said?

I am beginning to think it's me. For the past few days, I have been re-reading *Harry Potter and The Philosopher's Stone* for a children's fiction month in Lush Places Book Club. And in the same way that when you read health information on the internet you are convinced you are seriously ill, I have suddenly developed the ability to understand a kind of

Parseltongue, the language of snakes and other magical creatures.

For example, the other day, when I was having licentious thoughts about Mr Grigg when he was spending a night away (because absence makes the heart grow fonder and we are getting on a little better these days), a huddle of teenage schoolgirls walked by singing '...Nothing can compare to your neighbourhood whore...' and then giggled off stage left.

Then, on Friday, I was recovering from two injections inflicted on me by an over-enthusiastic dentist. It was on the NHS so I won't complain. Afterwards, I agreed to go for a walk with Pelly Sheepwash on the understanding I wouldn't talk. You try saying 'specific' and 'balsam' when your top lip and tongue feel like they have been lashed by 50,000 stinging nettles. Pelly kindly resisted the temptation to call me 'Duck Face' and I began to overcome my self-pity. And then several children on their way to the football ground walked by. A particularly annoying boy, who looks like an angel but has a mouth like an ash tray, looked at me, grinned and said: 'Sshh, are you sheerious?' I hadn't even opened my mouth.

So when we walked through the yard of the farmer on the hill that is occasionally visited by aliens, I felt for sure he would speak my language. You know, along the lines of the farmer from *Hot Fuzz* who, translated by a rustic police officer, turns out to have an arsenal in his outbuildings.

I grinned, not realising I looked like John Mills in his Oscar-winning role in *Ryan's Daughter* crossed with Orville and said: 'Schtill warmisch for thisch time of year, ishtn't it?'

He looked at me as if I were the village idiot.

He turned to Pelly and said, in the perfect accent of an English gentleman: 'Nice weather for ducks, isn't it?'

21 October: This morning, as I walk the spaniels around the field, I hear the ghost of Russell's Crow shrieking in the hen coop across the valley. The sun comes up over the beech wood on Bluebell Hill. The summit of its flat-topped sibling across the way grows in silhouette.

The secondary school children saunter down to the school bus, singing some inappropriate pop song as they pass The Extremely Pleasant Company, a stationery business run from the old telephone exchange.

It is quiet here in Lush Places but it's been a busy weekend. The applause is still ringing in my ears after the harvest supper organised by Mrs Bancroft and the Parson's Daughter. They can congratulate themselves on a fine evening of entertainment in the village hall. Who needs West End theatres when we have an elderly farmer on the piano, playing the right notes but not necessarily in the right order? And a child prodigy playing *Moonlight Sonata*? The village stalwarts, Mr and Mrs Pope, doing a modern take on Nelson's last moments, complete with diversity, health and safety restrictions and EC laws? And a rousing finale of risqué jokes by Celebrity Farmer before he donned a mask and moonwalked to Michael Jackson's *Thriller*?

My own contribution was a poem by my late uncle, George Withers:

The Land Remains
I remember - I remember the place where I was born;
'Twas full of cows and heifers then, and sheep and pigs

and corn.
But the country scene is changing; the folks are changing too,
And farming's very different from the farming that I knew.

No geese are on the village green, no ponies are on the moors,
No cock crows on the dunghill now, the hens are all indoors,
The school's become a second home, the pub is closing down,
And the village shop just can't compete with Tesco's in the town.

The dairy herd is long dispersed, the quota's out on lease,
And the farmhouse sold to clear the debts and please the mortgagees;
And Father drives a lorry now, and Mum does B&Bs
In a semi on the new estate beyond the churchyard trees.

And there's new folk in the old place now; I don't know what they do,
But he's something in computers and a real nice fellow too.
They come to village functions; she's joined the W.I.;
They've not much clue as to what to do, but it must be said, they try!

Now the garden's gravelled over – it's a TV gardener's dream
With flowers in terracotta pots and a switch-on wildlife stream;

The rockery's a mockery of what was there before,
And the polystyrene staddle stones - well, they're the final straw!

No rows of spuds and carrots now, no runner beans and peas,
No cabbages, no rhubarb, no children climbing trees.
There's a four bi' four for Daddy and an Audi for his wife;
There's lots of Country Living - but no real country life!

But dawn still rises in the East, the sun still sinks in the West;
We come, we try, we live, we die, we work, we eat, we rest,
But love or hate the system, whoever holds the reins,
Let others learn – we've had our turn - and still the land remains.

23 October: It is cold and frosty in Lush Places. This morning, ribbons of mist lie in the valleys like trails of whipped-up egg white. And tonight, the nymph statue that welcomes visitors to the village ought to be wearing a hat, scarf and gloves.

Up at the community room, Mr Putter is reprimanded for a tuneful burst of *Where have all the young men gone.*

Caruso makes a knife motion across his throat and shouts: 'Cut!'

It is choir practice night and Mr Putter is feeling confident. Mr Grigg, who has only been to one singing session and is still to be convinced he has a decent voice, is away. Night Nurse is scolded again for losing her place, while I forget a dotted note and someone else is blamed for the clashing of voices. Sometimes it is good to be teacher's pet.

'I remember performing at The Albert Hall,' Caruso says, 'I was singing Haydn's *Creation*. The old dear next to me was singing Handel's *Messiah*.'

He raps his harmonica and calls for order.

We need to be in fine voice for a performance just before Christmas when our Enchanted Village voices will join Ding Dong Daddy and his friends for a special concert. It is incredible how ideas casually tossed around the pub turn into full-blown events. It's how we work.

Meanwhile, we have a special appearance at the old folk's home to worry about. As if we are in detention, the top team of six stay behind to practise *The Coventry Carol*. It is so beautifully moving it makes my cheekbones ache.

After my cold last week, I struggle to reach the top notes and to sustain the melody right to the end. And when I get home, alone, the Medea Necklace threatens to engulf me.

Where is Mr Grigg when I need him?

26 October: The clocks go back on Sunday. It happens every year. And every year it causes chaos in Lush Places.

'Is it backwards or forwards?' Mr Grigg asks.

'Spring forward, fall backwards,' I say, repeating the oft-heard mantra that ripples the length and breadth of Britain twice a year. Although why you can't fall forward is beyond me. Tell that to someone who has just plunged head-first down the stairs.

Anyway, I digress.

Most people hate the clocks going back. It's the official end to British Summer Time. The only good thing is an extra hour in bed.

But I love it. It means cosy warm nights by the fire and slightly lighter mornings, which makes all the difference when you are walking two excited spaniels at six forty-five through a pitch-black field.

'Are you sure?' Mr Grigg asks. 'Won't it be darker?'

'No,' I say, patiently. 'It's spring forwards, fall backwards, remember?'

'Yes, but doesn't that mean the mornings will get darker?'

'No,' I say, wondering how this usually intelligent man is unable to get his head around the clocks-changing concept.

Although at this time of year in Lush Places, it seems to be forever *Groundhog Day*. Puzzled looks, shrugs, is-it-backwards-or-forwards-type questions in the pub, people turning up an hour late for Sunday lunch – nothing is quite so confusing for us here than the weekend the clocks go back.

Unless you happen to be in our village hall. Last weekend, after a particularly riotous party, the guests sober enough to notice were alarmed to see the clock reach one and then suddenly hurtle backwards at breakneck speed.

There was a cheer from the drunken ones among us who got ready to party all over again.

We were a little disappointed to find out later that the clock does this every night to wind itself up. Wind itself up? Wind us up more like.

31 October: There has been a rush on pumpkins at the local nursery for a Halloween competition in the village hall. The gardens and allotments society, in an attempt to get more people interested, put on the event for its AGM last night. We are not members but Nobby Odd-Job is and to show our support for him, we turned up with our pumpkin lantern to add to the table of entries at the back. My Lidl pumpkin, carved on Wednesday, had become quite soft and its once wide open mouth and crooked teeth had shut after the top lip sank into its chin.

The committee, combined aged nine hundred and twenty six, was dressed in pointy hats and wizard cloaks as we settled down to listen to our guest speaker (and pumpkin judge) talk about dowsing and healing. The surreal picture of elderly, normally upstanding, Christian members of the community, sitting in rows in the hall dressed as witches, was quite unsettling. It reminded me of a Harry Potter convention. And when the guest speaker started talking to her dowsing rods and stroking her crystals, it dawned on the committee she was actually a white witch. Quite appropriate really, given the date, but none of them had realised this at the time of booking.

Meanwhile, the pumpkins at the back were getting hotter and the smell of burning became too strong to politely ignore. As the speaker got the energy flowing through her dowsing rods, my earring flew off and two pumpkins suddenly burst into flames. The smoke detectors, however, failed to pick this up, having been boxed in with cereal packets for Celebrity Farmer's Thriller dance routine which had involved smoke bombs and explosions.

Fortunately, the speaker found a ready supply of water (her rods took her to the kitchen sink) and gave the offending pumpkins a good soaking. That wiped the cheerful grins off their faces.

Drama over, we tucked in to a hearty supper and then realised we were the only ones drinking alcohol. Flyers had been sent around the village, inviting people to bring their own liquid refreshment and glasses. We took this to mean red wine, but everyone else had brought fruit juice or cordial and some had brought nothing at all. We felt like alcoholics at a temperance meeting.

Somehow, we were persuaded to stay for the AGM ('it won't last long,' our friend said, 'only a couple of hours'. We thought he was joking).

Half an hour later, and stalemate having been reached on whether the society should remove the word 'allotments' from its title after a schism in the ranks ('they don't want anything to do with us' was the widely-held view), we sloped off to the pub.

Chapter 11

November

1 November: It is All Souls Day and in about an hour's time I have to lock up the church as a favour to the usual key master, Nobby Odd-Job. I really need to check it first for tramps sleeping under pews before I turn the key. I'd best take a torch with me. It is very dark down here.

The rain is coming down in sheets here on All Souls Day. The empty square is a contrast to last night when the village was buzzing with skeletons, witches, Frankenstein monsters and some children as just plain hoodies.

Trick or Treat in this village is quite a civilised, good natured affair. The children are accompanied by parents or older siblings and call only at those houses where they know they will be welcomed.

Meanwhile, back at the Grigg hovel, Mr Grigg had his own ideas about tricking or treating. When the young visitors knocked on our door, he would ask what trick they'd like. Tiring of the fact they didn't seem to get the joke, he went one step further, ready for the next lot.

'What are you doing?' I asked, as he whipped an old duvet cover from the airing cupboard.

'Just wait and see.'

With that, he got out the scissors, made some appropriate holes and, hey presto, alakazam, izzy whizzy let's get busy, an apparition arose in our front hall.

Mr Grigg became Caspar the unfriendly ghost. And that, coupled with a water pistol and a stuffed fox's head with bared teeth. seemed to do the trick.

We weren't bothered again.

2 November: You can tell winter is coming because of all the stupid Christmas catalogues coming through the letterbox, the Yellow Pages propped up outside in a plastic bag (does anyone use Yellow Pages anymore?), the mud-splattered cars, walking the dogs in the dark, the smell of woodsmoke from the village chimney pots, Mr Loggins resuming his seasonal chainsaw massacre and the coal lorry parked in the middle of the Square.

But most of all you can tell it is winter because Mr Grigg is on the green cabbage soup diet again. Everyone knows it's windy.

3 November: I have been at the Death Star again today. Refurbishment is going on in one of the wings and there were tapping noises coming from the radiators. Probably local government workers trapped in the system, trying to escape.

I shall be heading down the escape tunnel myself at the end of the month. I have been editing web copy for three days a week for the past five months. It was a temporary job which was meant to be for six weeks. I feel a mixture of relief and anxiety at the prospect of seeing the light again. Relief because I shall at last be escaping my silo for the big wide world. But also anxiety because there will be very little money in the family purse for a while.

But I have been at the Death Star for too long. In my first week, I kept hearing the phrase 'customer engagement'. I now realise my colleagues meant 'talking to people'. For months, I have been trying to make my way through public sector gobbledegook, which is like wading through treacle with hobnail boots on and both legs tied together.

I have been horizon scanning, worrying about resource allocation, external challenges and improvement levers; holistic governance, coterminosity and predictors of beaconicity.

Gobbledegook? Bollocks more like.

Today, the Local Government Organisation issued a list of 100 words it wants to see banned in the public sector. For 'slippage' read 'delay', for 'funding streams' read 'money' and for 'core message' read 'main point'. Will the LGO's advice be taken on board and change the way public sector organisations speak to us, the public? Will it hell as like.

A more simple life beckons for me, working from home where impenetrable language is banned because neither the spaniels nor Mr Grigg nor I for that matter understand it. Days when I can take the dogs out for an hour and still be at my home office desk by eight thirty. Penniless but rich beyond measure.

Today, Mr Grigg rang me from home to ask if I still had the estimate for the fencing on the village green. The contractor had just started the work across the Square and then thought he had better knock on the door. '*How* much was that estimate I gave you?' he said. 'Only I don't want to charge the hall committee too much.'

Country life. I wouldn't have it any other way.

14 November: A tattered St George's flag ripples on top of the church. It is early morning and a regiment of rooks descends on the stays of the flagpole, sinister, like something from Alfred Hitchcock's *The Birds*.

The pink-tinged clouds signal the arrival of Homer's rosy fingered dawn and The Enchanted Village awakes, twinkling lights coming on up and along the valley to a theme of *The Planet Suite* on my iPod.

Autumn has well and truly arrived.

At Mr and Mrs Champagne-Charlie's, a bumper parcel arrives, stashed with fireworks. These are the ones Mr Grigg and his pals will be setting off on Friday evening to celebrate Bonfire Night. The crowds will be thronging the square, queuing up for burgers and hot dogs, going 'ooh' and 'ahh' in all the right places when Nobby Odd-Job and Mr Sheepwash light the blue touchpaper and Mr Grigg and I will stand well back as the rockets zoom up over the village green and land far away rather than on the church roof and blocking the guttering like they did last year. Or the previous year, when all the rocket tails ended up spiked neatly in individual graves.

The ginger wig blows by like tumbleweed as I make my way up to the old people's complex for our weekly singing session. Caruso is in fine form, splitting us up into basses, altos and sopranos to sing *Good King Wenceslas* in rounds.

We are just getting up a good head of steam when he raps his baton and stops us mid-flow. Our voices are a derailed train, tumbling into the sidings. He shouts, wildly.

'I'm only going to say this once. Don't miss out that dotted note.'

Our sniggers stifled, he starts us up again. We're in fine form, steaming and a rolling through crisp and even snow and gathering winter fu-el. And then the train hits the buffers.

'Sopranos [that's me], you're dropping the pitch!'

We look down at our sheet music, not daring to even take a glance at each other. I sneak a peep, like you might sometimes do in church to see if other people are really praying. Mr and Mrs Putter are going cross-eyed, the Parson's Daughter is suppressing a giggle and Mamma Mia is looking very perplexed. Night Nurse looks defiant and Mrs Regal Bird has the face of an angel.

And then, at the end, Caruso announces the line-up for his dream team for a singsong at the village's old people's home in December.

And I'm in it.

8 November: The winds roared through the night, as the windows were lashed with heavy rain. This morning there are puddles everywhere. A thick, brown gilet of sycamore and beech leaves lines the windscreen and bonnet of a parked car, keeping the vehicle warm until it awakes.

The weather held out for bonfire night and the skies around The Enchanted Village were a riot of colour as Mr Grigg set off rockets with names like 'Explorer' and 'Goliath'. As well as our own village do, the posh people up the road pitched in, with fireworks even bigger and better than we commoners could afford.

Over the hill, the sky lit up from north to south, from east to west, with flashes of light accompanied by loud booms. For one night only, World War Three had been declared.

And in the pub and several pints of cider later, Mr Putter led a small table in a singsong, starting with Donald *Where's Yer Troosers*. Mr Grigg lowered the tone, with a cheeky rendition of Adge Cutler and The Wurzels' *Twice Daily*.

And then the landlady got down the hunting horns again. We hadn't seen anything like this since Dudley's wake back in the summer.

We found ourselves being conducted in ten verses of *Roll Me Over in the Clover*, rapidly followed by me leading *Dinah, Dinah Show Us Yer Leg*. Even the usually ladylike Mrs Bancroft was chuckling and joining in, while the fragrant Mrs Putter managed to get a very good tune out of one of the horns, although not half as good as the landlady, who must surely have been a whipper-in in a previous life.

The saving grace was that our singing master, Caruso, wasn't in the pub that night. He would have been worried about more than just our intonation. The words might have vexed him slightly too.

Roll me over in the clover indeed.

18 November: Jupiter shines like a beacon in the southern sky. There is an eerie halo around a waxing gibbous moon. This circle of ice crystals disappears as the clouds make way for the moon to throw its ghostly light across fields and hedges.

Bright stars are revealed, studding the heavens like sparkling eyes. Lyra and Cygnus, Cassiopeia and Andromeda. Mythical names in faraway places. We are tiny. Specks in a massive universe.

The Enchanted Village is still tonight, in mourning for two good souls who are no longer with us. Our wise former neighbour, Gandalf, once so active and skilful, who gradually became old and weary and was ready to go. Every time I walk in my kitchen I see him in my mind, fitting my cupboard and plastering a wall when he was eighty years old and running around like a man half his age.

And then the sad, sad passing of our shopkeeper, a woman not much older than me, who died suddenly on holiday. She was far too young to go. A serene, kind person, a hard worker who did not deserve to be taken so soon.

Two more stars join the heavens.

Chapter 12

December

1 December: Our thoughts are on a poignant funeral for a friend.

A cold church, puffs of steam coming from people's mouths and noses as they sing *Amazing Grace*, a floral tribute that says 'Mum', a tolling bell and memories of a feisty, fun and pint-sized woman loved by all who knew her. The church is packed with villagers, in big coats and warm hats. They stand in the pews: Caruso, Super Mario and his new wife, Princess Peach, the Popes, the Parson's Daughter, Nobby Odd-Job, Mamma Mia, Mr and Mrs Sheepwash and Mrs Bancroft. There is Night Nurse, there is Posh Totty, MDF Man, Mr F Word and Camilla and Mr and Mrs Putter. The church is so full that Tuppence and Ding Dong Daddy and his wife have to sit in the choir stalls, just steps away from our departed friend.

She leaves the church to a soundtrack of sobs, sad faces and Leonard Cohen singing *Hallelujah*.

It is the first day of advent, a time when our thoughts are usually about the lead-up to Christmas. But it is hard when you see so much grief around you.

Later, we share joyous moments with the family in the village hall. With plates of vol-au-vents, sandwiches and coffee cake, cups of tea and glasses of wine, we watch a slide show featuring pictures of our shopkeeper and then a BBC film made for *The Politics Show* about declining village services. The Enchanted Village looks truly enchanting, with camera shots through redundant pumps and hanging baskets into the misty streets beyond. And there is our shopkeeper, putting out the fresh flowers. She is a tiny slip of a thing, surrounded by colourful chrysanthemums.

3 December: On the way to the Big House, Caruso's choir clutch their sheets of music. Emotions are running high because of the funeral and wake we have just attended. There is trepidation in the air. Will Night Nurse find the right music? Will The Parson's Daughter and I clash with the altos in *I Saw a Maiden*? Will Mr Putter get his longed-for solo?

We disrobe in the dining room, leaving our music folders behind, taking just the sheets we need for the afternoon's performance. The sitting room of the old people's home is lined with residents, most of whom look pleased to see us. Mr Putter says a cheerful hello to a lady in a wheelchair who mutters: 'Stupid people.'

Our reputation precedes us.

So we chug along, singing joyfully, and get into our stride. Caruso struggles to find the correct sheet for his solo (the irony of which does not go unnoticed by Night Nurse and also Mr Putter, who thinks he is in with a chance of a solo). And then when he introduces the next number, a resident is heard to say: 'Oh no, not another bloody song.'

At the end of our performance, Caruso tells them we'll be back again in a few weeks' time.

'Well, I'm going out on that day then,' says a resident with limited mobility.

Another, who was joining in the chorus of *Dashing Away with the Smoothing Iron*, smiles as if to say: 'Take no notice, we enjoyed it.'

As we put on our hats and coats for the walk back into the village, a look of terror crosses Mr Putter's face when he put his hand into his music folder and pulls out sheets marked up for a soprano. Someone has walked off with his music. In amongst all the 'official' songs are ones he had printed off from the internet, including *Donald Where's Yer Troosers.* His cunning plan to come out with a surprise solo of his own at the Christmas supper in the pub has been well and truly scuppered.

5 December: Christmas is on its way. The Enchanted Village's version of *Last of The Summer Wine* is huddled under the teenage shelter drinking coffee and eating toast.

There's Mr Champagne-Charlie with flat cap on as Foggy, Mr Sheepwash with wry observations on life as Clegg and Mr Grigg and Nobby Odd-Job doing a double act as Compo. Nobby is wearing the Compo hat but Mr Grigg is wearing the Compo mouth, stating the crude and obvious.

They are on the village green, putting up the Christmas tree lights. The power comes from a hole in the tree - magic, see? - where the Punch and Judy man normally plugs in his microphone on village fete day.

The Enchanted Village mist swirls as Celebrity Farmer and his father meet each other on tractors where the ley lines cross in the square. They wave to me as if it is quite normal for me to be walking across the village square in a colourful apron and carrying a tray of spotted coffee cups.

Next to the village pump, a white van has broken down, and there are ball bearings all over the square. I fear a cartoon comedy moment coming on.

But it passes. And life resumes as normal.

9 December: This evening, just before sunset, woodsmoke wafts from the chimneys, creating a long, low, white cloud running the length of the village. Cars are iced up, the grass is frosting and I pray for snow in the morning so I don't have to go into the office.

10 December: But my prayers are not answered. However, there are some advantages to being in the rat race. I hate getting up in the dark and going home in the dark. But the beauty of the skies in December is breathtaking. This morning, a Homeresque dawn greets me as I drive past the BBC transmitting station, that modern take on Stonehenge, metal mast icons for the Age of Aquarius. And then this evening. Venus is a brilliant diamond in the south west at dusk, following Jupiter down as the evening wears on. It is a joy to drive home towards them. And then, as I walk the dogs, I realise I don't need the torch. The Oak Moon, or Snow Moon, is on its way, rising high above three beech trees in the hedgerow. Absolutely stunning. I stop and take it all in, breathe in the cold air and smell the woodsmoke. I thank God I am healthy and alive.

According to the wonderful *Stargazers' Almanac,* given to me by the boffin who runs the mobile planetarium, we will be able to see Saturn at midnight during the middle of the month and then Mercury next to the moon in the west at dusk on 29 December.

I once borrowed a telescope and was spellbound by the craters of the moon. From the warmth of my conservatory, it was like being at the helm of the Millennium Falcon.

I think I would like a telescope for Christmas.

11 December: So I find myself at the office Christmas party, surprisingly sober, and watching the dramas unfolding around me: acres of flesh on display, flesh that would be better housed under a nice little bolero jacket, legs up to armpits and people who usually wear glasses suddenly small-eyed and slightly scared looking as they witness the spectacle in contact lenses. There is pent-up passion, hands-on knees-under-tables, a look, a glance, sighing, raised voices, ladies bopping wistfully to *Dancing Queen* and someone from IT getting up to applause for *Sex Machine.*

I smile inside, above all this predictable chicanery. I excuse myself and go to the ladies, where colleagues are yelling to each other from the cubicles.

I look in the mirror as I wash my hands and wonder at it all. Here I am, nearly fifty, and scenes from the school disco whizzing past in cinematic montage.

A rather well-built woman comes out fresh from flushing.

'Excuse me, love,' she says.

I bristle, sensing a fight. Had I inadvertently looked at her husband?

'Not being funny but...'

She's moving in for the kill and she says: 'Well, it might be the fashion...'

And then I realise. I have just committed the classic Ladies Toilets Faux Pas.

'You've got your dress tucked into your knickers.'

12 December: At the entrance to the Enchanted Village, the bronze nymph statue is wearing her winter garb of chequered poncho and a bobble hat to keep out the cold winds that funnel down through the one-way system.

So this is Christmas.

15 December: This morning, as the rooks flew sideways, buffeted against the wind, I reflected on one of those very surreal weekends that seem to happen only in this village.

It began in the pub on Friday night where the chrome pole was wedged twixt floor and ceiling, in readiness for a girls' night out involving a group of ladies including Mrs Bobby Packman, Randy Munchkin and Mrs Monty Chocs-Away. But there were no takers and the pole stood gleaming in splendid isolation, although Larry the Landlord was thinking about it, as he unbuttoned his shirt behind the bar and kissed his own shoulder. When the door opened and Posh Totty walked in, I saw Mr Grigg and Nobby Odd-Job's eyes light up. But the moment was fleeting, as she was quickly followed by her husband and family.

During the course of the evening, Larry was talking to customers at a table near the fire. The Fragrant Mrs Putter, tired of waiting for a drink, walked behind the bar and pulled her own pint. Larry was behind her in an instant, and became Patrick Swayze to her Demi Moore on the potter's wheel in *Ghost*.

Picture it. The caption could have been: 'A glass of wine? I've got a nice semillion.'

The next day, Mr Grigg went beating and came back dirty, wet and sweaty, twenty minutes before the school Christmas Fair was about to start. Not long after he had a dressing down from me, a handbell was heard clanging around the one-way system. The red-hooded figure of Santa suddenly materialised in the churchyard, sitting on a quadbike driven by Celebrity Farmer's dad.

After the fair was over, Santa was spotted delivering a brace of pheasants next door.

'You're meant to go down the chimney,' yelled a group of passing children.

He was greeted by Champagne-Charlie, strutting around in plus-fours, who at supper that evening did an exceptional imitation of Rowley Birkin QC from *The Fast Show* without even realising it.

The next day, after breakfast in the village hall, Mr Grigg and I went to Clarks Village in Street to do some Christmas Shopping. Strangely, we kept seeing ladies from our village darting in and out of *Eastex* and *Le Creuset*. It was like something from an episode of *The Prisoner* or the film *Don't Look Now*. It transpired they were killing time before going to see Pam Ayres at the Strode Theatre.

Back at home, Mr Grigg took it upon himself to pluck six partridges on the dining room table, just as Pelly Sheepwash, a vegetarian, arrived for supper with her husband. We finished off cracking wet walnuts with our bare hands because the nut crackers were broken.

It's a strange old life.

16 December: As the choir sits down to its Christmas meal in the pub, Caruso, with festive hat at a jaunty angle, fumbles around with his music.

'I think it's time we had a song,' he says.

Quick as mustard, Mr Putter steps up to the podium, rapidly dishing out photocopied sheets bearing the immortal words of *Donald Where's Yer Troosers*.

We all join in, much too low, and Caruso's face is like thunder. He was thinking more along the lines of a tuneful *The Holly and The Ivy* in rounds.

The pub rapidly empties of customers.

We fear people with tickets for our concert at the weekend might soon be asking for a refund.

And then, like a saviour, Caruso redeems us all with a beautiful rendition of William Butler Yeats' poem, *He Wishes for the Cloths of Heaven*, in song.

Mr Putter makes an emotional speech about how much he has enjoyed our singing evenings, expresses his deep love for Caruso (but not in a weird way as he squeezes the knee of his fragrant wife) and we all applaud.

Caruso thanks me, of all people, because I persuaded him to revive the choir at Dudley's wake.

We raise our glasses to dear Dudley's memory, a wine bottle falls over – rather like Dudley used to after too many glasses of Grand Marnier – and then Caruso sneezes five times in a row.

20 December: It was all building up to a crescendo. We were so looking forward to our big moment with the choir and Ding Dong Daddy's friends. And then it came.

Deep and crisp and even.

For the past few days, we have been up to our necks in snow. Across the land, we're feeling The Grinch's icy pinch. Oil stocks are running low, trains are being cancelled and freezers are being raided for fruit and veg sensibly put in during a summer glut.

We made our way to a carol concert at the Big House, walking along the snowy driveway, brushstrokes in a Brueghel painting, illuminated by a waxing gibbous moon.

Mr Putter sang his longed-for solo when Caruso threw him a verse for *We Three Kings*, with Caspar landing in his lap, at the last minute. There was a round of applause when he finished, in time and on tune. And then the concert we had all been waiting for, practising for, singing for, was upon us. But because of the snow, it was cancelled.

So it was off to the pub for scampi and chips and an impromptu folk session featuring Ding Dong Daddy and friends, including the 2010 international solo jig champion.

As the dancer bounced up and down to *The Bluebell Polka*, flicking a leg here, and a white hanky there, the stuffed stag's head gazed down, unfazed by the Christmas bells and shiny baubles hanging from its antlers.

Lush Places: truly an enchanted village.

23 December: The tree above the Grigg hovel is flashing like something from New York's Times Square.

'We've had complaints' says Mrs Bancroft, the owner of a beautifully arranged Christmas tree on the corner of her house. The tree is a wonderful shape and the lights are perfect. Just like her.

As I stand gawping in the square, Mr Grigg pulls up from five hours of Christmas shopping in Bridport and a swift pint in the only free house for miles around.

'What's wrong with the bloody tree?' he says, like it's my fault. 'It's bloody flashing.'

I sit in the bedroom window looking out at the lights as he tries to sort out the switches on the plug in the socket near the floor.

'Sequence, chasing, glow, completely still,' he yells at me but looking at the plug.

'They're completely out, honestly,' I say. I look out the window wishing I were somewhere warm and light. 'There's nothing happening, nothing.'

He gets up to look and the lights come back on again. He scoffs, thinking I'm making it up. We try again and the same thing happens. Every time he looks away the lights go off. Every time he looks they behave. The next time he keeps an eye on the lights and the other eye on the socket.

The lights fail.

'You're right,' he says. He sounds surprised.

We struggle to adjust the lights to static but they're having none of it. Our tree is a beacon of activity in an otherwise static and sedate square. The Grigg household flashes like billio while around us all the other lights are keeping their heads. We seem to be losing ours. But we're all right. We just close the curtains. What the eye doesn't see...

From the Bancroft household across the road, our lights perform a cabaret. Mrs Bancroft and her family close the curtains before putting on the eye shades.

This one could run and run. All over the festive period.

26 December: The day started so well. Christmas Day in The Enchanted Village. Pillowcases stuffed full of presents: new socks, Ferrero Rocher, a personalised calendar of our travels.

A bird-within-a-bird-within-a-bird, courtesy of Mr Champagne-Charlie next door, who had bagged four of the six birds before turning them into a culinary creation for us. Cranberry sauce prepared Gordon Ramsay-style, Louis Prima on the stereo and then the bottle of champagne.

Looking back, that's where it all started to go wrong. Niggling rows with Mr Grigg as we prepared the veg at the kitchen island, the disappointment at a new pair of boots a half size too small and then the decision to wander over to the pub for just the one drink while the bird-within-a-bird cooked merrily in the Aga.

Two hours and five drinks later, Mr Grigg's younger brother and two children wandered into the pub. We staggered out to go home, the cold air hit me and I was out for the count.

This morning, on Boxing Day, I have just had a slice of cold bird-within-a-bird and a cold roast parsnip. It was obviously a lovely meal. A great time was had by all.

It's just a shame I missed it.

27 December: Mr Grigg disappeared again today. I know it's the season of goodwill and all but he's been doing this disappearing act for nearly a year and I'm getting mighty fed up with it.

30 December: The day before New Year's Eve and the shops in Bridport are heaving.

Mr Grigg and I go from Lidls to Morrisons, shadowed by a gabbling gipsy family looking for bargains on the salmonella shelf. Mr Grigg hovers closely behind them, puts in a hand and pulls out a tray of pigs in blankets.

'That'll do for tomorrow night,' he says, plucking two half price pork pies and a packet of twelve loaded potato skins from the refrigerated unit.

He pulls away from the crowd, the spoils under his arm. The gipsy family look suitably impressed.

I struggle to find prunes and cocktail sticks and go back and forth, passing a man who smells like he hasn't had a wash in years who is pondering over whether to buy a 'value' pack of digestives to go with his two tins of new potatoes.

After the fifth time of wandering up and down the same aisles, I finally ask a disinterested man stacking shelves. He mutters to himself as if he's remembering the winning numbers of the lottery from a dream. At last he says: 'Aisles fourteen and fifteen', without even giving me eye contact. Yet when Mr Grigg asks for the condensed milk, a rather large female assistant smiles and says: 'follow me', seduction written all over her full moon face.

Mr Grigg is a charmer, a man with whom men want to get drunk and women fall in love.

I shall be watching him closely this New Year's Eve, and staying very sober.

31 December: I struggle into a red basque and put my left foot, encased in a long, laced boot, on the side of the bed.

'Can you help me with my bodice?' I ask, as Mr Grigg sashays over and looks at himself in the mirror. He is wearing a large black Stetson, a white shirt, black waistcoat, trousers and jacket, with a couple of playing cards (aces of course) sticking out from his pocket. He looks like James Garner as *Bret Maverick*, which I think is very apt. He has been practising his 'drawing' technique, to see how quickly he can get out his replica Colt .44 bought from the joke shop just a few hours earlier.

I hoist my long black skirt up over my knees and stand firm as Mr Grigg pulls my strings.

'This,' he says, 'suits you very much. Can you keep it on when we come home?'

'Yes,' I say, 'but I'm taking this bloody necklace off. I've had enough of it.'

The Medea Necklace is flung to the floor, buttons crashing everywhere. I feel a new sense of freedom. He is not going to get me down. I must be more confident.

On our way up to the village hall, we are joined by an assortment of cowboys and indians as the party theme is 'Wild West'. Champagne-Charlie has his Winchester rifle strapped across this shoulder, Bubbles is dressed as Calamity Jane, Mrs Bancroft is an upmarket saloon keeper, Mr and Mrs Sheepwash are a couple of strays from the Blackfoot tribe and the fragrant Mrs Putter is Pocahontas, with Mr Putter cutting a dash as Captain John Smith.

We walk into the hall to the sound of the theme from *The Virginian*. Mr Grigg is more of a *Bonanza* man really but is still in his element.

Posh Totty, who has come as Annie Oakley, saunters across and looks at Mr Grigg in a knowing way. He smiles that moon smile and, if it were not for an announcement that the games are about to begin, there could quite easily have been a showdown.

He spends rather too long in a clinch with a couple of balloons and a pretty saloon girl and then, a few games of poker later, we line up for karaoke, with the girls jostling for position at the microphone. I am sulking with Mr Grigg doing all that clinching so I watch from the sidelines, drowning my sorrows in a large glass of Sauvignon Blanc as they break out into *Right By Your Side* by The Eurythmics, led by Tuppence on whoop-whoops and whistles.

I feel their words are directed at me. I look across at Mr Grigg, still in animated conversation with one of his fans on the other side of the hall. I stomp across, in my laced-up boots as Pelly programmes *Jackson* into the karaoke machine, her reading glasses perched on the end of her nose. I grab Mr Grigg, give him a microphone and I become June Carter to his Johnny Cash. We serenade each other, standing four square, the room whirling around us. I can see out of the corner of my eye Champagne-Charlie tapping his feet as Mr Loggins pretends to play the guitar.

And then it turns into *Suspicious Minds* and Mr and Mrs Sheepwash become Elvis and Pricilla Presley.

It goes on like that until someone notices that the big hand on the clock above the stage is fast approaching midnight. I look around and realise Mr Grigg is nowhere to be seen.

The party stampedes from the hall and down the village green for the New Year's Eve countdown. The heels of my boots spike the grass as I try to make it to the square before the clock stops chiming. It strikes twelve (although it could be thirteen) as the cast of enchanted village characters snakes down from the hall past the play equipment to the tune of *Locomotion*, by Little Eva, coming from the jukebox in the pub where more revellers are spilling out to mark the New Year.

There are two lines. Us and them. The ones from the hall and the ones from the pub. Pioneers and assorted Native American tribes, ready to fight. When Hawkeye comes out from the pub, shouting 'Happy New Year' in his Dorset John Wayne drawl, closely followed by Mr St John yelling a war cry and brandishing a rubber machete, I fear there might be a shoot-out.

And then Caruso starts singing *Auld Lang Syne*. We link arms, all of us, a huge great circle in the square. We sing, we slowly stomp towards each other, our hands intertwined. A taxi pulls up and has to wait as Lush Places comes together in a spirit of one-ness. We get faster and faster, meeting in the middle until the end of the song when there are kisses and hugs all round.

I see Bellows Packman embracing Mrs Champagne-Charlie, Darling Loggins cuddling Nobby Odd-Job, Pelly Sheepwash cosying up to Randy Munchkin and MDF Man and Mrs Bancroft hugging the fragrant Mrs Putter.

They kiss me but I feel alone. There is no sign of Mr Grigg.

And then there's a clatter of hooves and a white horse comes thundering down the one-way system.

My big bear of a husband is sitting astride it.

The horse comes to a halt. Mr Grigg calmly dismounts, adjusts his chaps and a huddle of ladies queue up for a New Year's kiss. Someone in the pub puts some money into the jukebox and Paolo Nutini's *Pencil full of Lead* springs into life. Mr Grigg looks up from the throng of women around him, shrugs his shoulders and mouths: 'I love you, baby.'

Posh Totty walks across to me in best *Annie Get Your Gun* mode, with her hands on her hips. I fear another fight coming on. It's about time I had it out with her. I should not be such a wimp.

'Didn't he do well?' she says.

'Well? What do you mean?' I can feel my hostility at last going out to greet the wider world. I have been sitting on these feelings for far too long.

'Darling, didn't you know?'

I can feel I am just about to punch here, but I am not sure how to even ball a fist.

Posh Totty comes closer to me.

She smiles as she says: 'I've been giving him riding lessons all year. He wanted to impress you. He absolutely adores you, you know.'

Feeling like the biggest fool in Christendom, I extend the hand of friendship.

'Bugger that, it's Christmas,' she says. 'Come and let me give you a hug.'

So we stand there, hugging like some long-lost friends who have found each other after years out in the cold.

'He's a top bloke, your man. You should be proud of him,' she says, as my hands touch her hair, which feels strangely artificial.

The ginger wig.

Around Lush Places, our very own enchanted village, the Christmas lights on our front door flash like they are going out of fashion, the Union flag over the shop is a-fluttering and the taxi driver waits patiently while we dance all around him.

This is a good place to be right now, I think, as John Lennon and *What Ever Gets You Through the Night* rings around the square.

Mr Grigg and I clinch like lovers on a film set.

'Happy new year, my love,' he whispers in my ear.

Epilogue

1 January: As the cast of the Enchanted Village slumbers in its beds, they are awoken abruptly by the sound of clashing sticks and screeching brakes. We stumble to our doors and windows in dressing gowns and pyjamas and look out across the square. The party poppers and streamers lie on the tarmac, like the tresses of an abandoned lover. A troupe of morris dancers stomps around the road in clogs, holding up the traffic and not caring a jot. A ginger wig sits, inert, at the road junction, like a squashed cat.

From our bedroom, we see Champagne-Charlie emerging from his front door, bleary eyed and with a hip flask. He looks up at our window and says to Mr Grigg: 'Fancy a snifter, chap?'

'I'm on my way,' Mr Grigg says, turning to go downstairs.

'Don't you think you ought to put some clothes on?' I say.

'Bugger that. Do I have to?' he says. 'It *is* New Year's Day.'

'Yes, Big Boy' I say, looking at this colossus of the man that is my husband. 'Let's start the year as we mean to go on.'

The End

Lightning Source UK Ltd.
Milton Keynes UK
UKOW05f0453151013
219055UK00001B/50/P